# THE GRUDGE

# THE GRUDGE

## Giles A. Lutz

GUNSMOKE

First published in the US by Doubleday

This hardback edition 2013
by AudioGO Ltd
by arrangement with
Golden West Literary Agency

ISBN 978 1 471 32056 9

British Library Cataloguing in Publication Data available.

Printed and bound in Great Britain by
MPG Books Group Limited

**Giles A[lfred] Lutz** was born in born in Kansas City, Missouri. He lived and worked in Missouri all his life. He worked as a rancher, breeding pedigreed Black Angus cattle, while he also wrote Western fiction for a wide variety of magazines, including *Lariat Story Magazine*, *Action Stories*, *Fifteen Western Tales*, and *Western Story*. The first of Lutz's eighty-two Western novels was *Fight or Run* (Popular Library. 1954). This and the succeeding nine novels published over a six-year period were all original paperbacks. In all, he published fifty such novels under his own name and various pseudonyms like Hunter Ingram and Reese Sullivan. With The *Honyocker* (Doubleday, 1961), Lutz began a long association with Doubleday, the publisher who would issue all but two of his hardcover novels. The *Honyocker* received the Spur Award as the best Western novel of 1961 from the Western Writers of America. Historical events and real people often figure in Lutz's novels, though few of the books qualify as historical novels in the usual sense. Perhaps the closest to this classification is *The Magnificent Failure* (Doubleday, 1967), which deals with Louis Tiel and the *Métis* rebellion in Montana and southern Canada in 1885. In other novels real events or people provide background or atmosphere but their treatment is subordinated to the needs of the main plot, as for example the use of Butch Cassidy's Hole-in-the-Wall gang in *Lure of the Outlaw Trail* (Doubleday, 1979). The best of Lutz's stories, including those under the Hunter Ingram byline, have an authentic Western atmosphere, fast action, credible characters, and a solidity and psychological truth that make them superior entertainment.

# THE GRUDGE

# CHAPTER ONE

The tall, angular man crossed his forearms and rested them on the saddle horn. "Sure you won't change your mind and leave with us, Gradie?" Munn North couldn't keep the hope out of his tone. Gradie Huston was one of the best men he had ever hired; he hated to even think of the possibility of losing him. Gradie said he would be along later, but so many things could happen to change his mind.

"I'm sure," Gradie said. "I'll follow you in a week or so." Probably sooner, he thought. He doubted that anything could hold him around Abilene long. His eyes never left the owner of the MN spread. That same intense gaze was an annoyance to many people.

North's horse twisted with impatience and gave a few tentative hops. They weren't actually bucks, but the horse was working himself up to cut loose.

North hauled the animal down with savage jerks on the reins. "Goddam you," he said plaintively. "Ain't I got enough on my mind without you acting up?" North's face was long and lean, the aging lines making it look severe. The humor in the cut of the mouth softened the rest of his features. Nobody ever accused him of being an unfair man.

"Damned horse's got more life than any of us," he grumbled.

The corners of Gradie's mouth twitched. That was sure the truth. The cattle were loaded on the cars, and North was taking his crew of ten men back to Texas. Gradie had never seen a more thoroughly wrung-out bunch. Abilene, Kansas, and its flesh-pots had demanded its full price in energy and money the last three nights. The bars, the tables, and the women had dipped in

1

rapacious claws and emptied the pockets of Munn North's men. Gradie would bet they couldn't raise two dollars' worth of change among them.

The crew sat slack in their saddles, their faces loose, their dull eyes showing their poverty of spirit. They were drained physically and mentally. Three months of hard work, long hours, and considerable risk were flung away in three nights of riotous living. Gradie thought sardonically, not a one of this bunch considered he bought himself a bad bargain. Only North would be taking any money back with him. North had the money from the sale of the cattle in his pockets.

Something was holding North here. Gradie wondered what it was. He waited patiently for North to speak.

North fidgeted, hating to give the order to move out. He wished he could talk Gradie out of whatever he had in his mind. North had the normal curiosity as to why Gradie was staying in Abilene. Was it a woman? Gradie sure hadn't given any indication of that. North hadn't seen him buy a single drink for a dance-hall girl, and some of those women weren't bad-looking, particularly to women-starved men. Gradie had just shrugged all of them away and continued on his way. In fact, North hadn't seen him spend much time around any of the saloons.

He would certainly like to know what was holding Gradie, but he had too much sense to pry. Gradie kept a hard shell about him that North never penetrated. He's worked for me three years, North thought, and I don't know him much better than the day he drifted in. North's judgment of Gradie Huston was formed the first day he saw him, and nothing had happened to change that opinion. Gradie was a loner; nobody would ever get to know him very well. He had a tremendous capacity for work, and he took on more than his share. Outside of work, Gradie didn't participate in much else. He hid behind that thick wall and turned aside every friendly approach.

Gradie looked at the man who meant more to him than his actual father. If there was anything to him, North had put it there. He had gone to work for North three years ago, an eighteen-year-old with little knowledge and not much more ability. He had wandered around for three years, accomplishing little and never staying long in one place. North had seen something in a scared and lonely kid, and gave Gradie a job that had broken the pattern of his aimless life. He taught Gradie everything, how to handle cattle and horses and how to use a gun. Gradie had supplied something to all that training, a natural speed and a cat's quick reflexes.

Gradie had never been able to say thanks. He had been so battered and beaten around in his earlier life that words came hard to him. No matter how badly he might want to say them, they stuck in his throat. North's other hands had given up early on him. They put him down as a strange one and left him pretty much to himself.

The silence between North and Gradie grew awkward. North sighed. Gradie was running from something. North guessed he would never find what it was now. He had the odd feeling that if Gradie didn't leave with them, he would never see him again. He searched his mind for the right words to reach Gradie, and they wouldn't come. There it is again, North thought; that wary watchfulness. It always appeared when Gradie thought he was being hemmed in by something. He reminded North of a big, red-tailed hawk, sitting on a high limb, not part of anything, but aware of everything that went on around him. North almost smiled. Hawk would have been a good name for Gradie. The fancy wasn't as farfetched as it sounded. North had seen Gradie's eyes become hard and fixed when he was intense about something. That was the way a hawk's eyes looked. North could almost swear Gradie's eyes had a yellow tinge to them now.

Men shifted restlessly in their saddles, and horses stomped impatiently. North knew that his hesitation was growing awkward, and he had to break up this moment.

He sighed and said, "So long, Gradie. If you ever need anything, you know where to find me."

"I'll sure keep that in mind," Gradie said gravely.

North raised his arm and whipped it forward. "Let's move," he bawled.

Twig and Hoadie lifted a hand toward Gradie in a farewell. The rest of them looked as though they couldn't care less.

Gradie stood there a long moment, watching the riders diminish in size. His loneliness grew until it threatened to overwhelm him. But that was nothing new. Even when he had a family, the loneliness had been there. Already, he was berating himself for the impulse that had prompted him to stay over in Abilene. He could get his horse from the livery stable and catch up with North and the bunch. He was strongly tempted.

Gradie swore at himself for this weakness. Rarely was he ever tormented by indecision, but he was now. It had been six years since he had seen Abilene, and if the railhead hadn't been driven to Abilene, he wouldn't be here now. He shook his head, a heavy scowl on his face. If he hadn't seen his mother yesterday afternoon, he would be gone with North now. He wished he hadn't come with North, he wished he hadn't seen Abilene again. Old scenes and memories began to clutch and pull at him the moment he rode into town. He had fought them off. His family lived just outside of town, and he had shut them out of his mind. As long as he had work to do he was all right. It wasn't so bad while the cattle were being loaded into the waiting cars. The bawling of the unhappy animals helped blot out his thinking.

But those old scenes and memories rushed back once the cattle were shipped. Then all he had to do was to wait out the time North had given his outfit to celebrate. Gradie could have gone through those three days, if he hadn't stepped out of his hotel yesterday afternoon.

He still saw Hannah Huston as plainly as though she stood before him. My God, she had looked so old, so worn-out. She shuffled out of Arnold's store, carrying a few pitiful packages. Gradie couldn't remember a time when she had enough money to buy more than the absolute necessities.

She had climbed heavily into that wreck of a buggy that looked as though it would fall down before the wheels made a complete revolution. The horse looked like all the animals the Hustons ever owned; a scarecrow of an animal with its backbone and ribs showing.

Gradie had plunged back into the Drovers' Cottage. His face was white, his eyes glazed. He had lived with that little voice before, accusing him of his guilt.

Sitting on his bed, Gradie stared at the far wall. It wasn't his fault, he repeated over and over. He had begged her to go with him, but Hannah refused to leave her husband. Maybe she had doubted a fourteen-year-old's ability to take care of her. How well Gradie remembered how he had raved at her. He couldn't do any worse than his father was doing.

Hannah had asked him a question that stopped him short in his tracks. "But how about Jonse, Gradie? What can I do about him?"

The memory of that moment clubbed Gradie with almost physical force. She couldn't do anything about Jonse. She couldn't take him with her, and she couldn't leave him. Jonse was only six and severely handicapped. His right arm was withered, and he hobbled painfully along on a club foot. Worse, he wasn't normal in the head. But he had a happy disposition, and he adored Gradie.

Gradie pounded a fist into his palm as all those old scenes trampled him under. He would ride out and see Hannah and Jonse in the morning, and give her what remained of his trail wages, only if she promised that his father and older brother never saw a cent of that money.

The old hating twisted his guts again. If he never saw his father and Phil again, nothing would please him more. All the earlier years of his life he had taken physical and spiritual abuse from those two. So he had run to escape them.

He shook his head, pulling himself back into the present. That was a part of his life that he would never really be able to escape. After he saw Hannah and Jonse, he would leave once more as he had six years ago. It was time he came to grips with reality. The feeling of guilt might always remain, but he wasn't going to be dragged down again into that particular kind of hell he had known too long.

Walking slowly down Texas Street, Grady knew he was only putting off riding out to the Huston place, because he was fearful of what he would see in Hannah's eyes. She would never put her accusation into words, but it would be in her eyes. You ran and left us, the silent accusation would scream at him.

Gradie writhed inwardly. Why didn't he just put the money in an envelope and send it out to her? Did he need for her to know who sent the money as an absolution for his guilt. It was more than that; he wanted to see her and Jonse. Maybe everybody would be better off, if he found a reason to shoot his father and Phil. He managed a wry grin. That was wishful thinking.

The arrival of the railroad in Abilene had stimulated the town's growth. Everywhere Gradie looked he saw evidence of new building. Houses sprawled to the north of the railroad, and substantial buildings lined the streets. When he lived here there hadn't been much to Abilene except Texas Street. Now new streets were laid out, and stores were erected all along them, too. The coming of the railroad was giving Abilene a heady taste of prosperity. A sour thought flashed through Gradie's mind. He could bet that the prosperity wouldn't touch the Hustons.

Most of the people he saw were strangers to him. Only two passed him that he knew, and they didn't give him a second look. Perhaps he had changed so that they didn't recognize him. He hadn't grown too much, for he wasn't a tall man. But he had filled out considerably, and there was a new confidence in his manner. He could remember when he walked down this street with his head hung low, ashamed of what he was and how he looked. That hangdog look was gone now. This was a new Gradie Huston who had returned to Abilene.

He passed the Bull Head's Saloon; one of the few familiar landmarks. The painting of the bull was still visible, though now faded. When that painting first appeared, it had aroused an indignant squawk from the women of Abilene. The painter had depicted the bull in all its pristine glory, and the women had gathered in furious groups talking about that disgraceful painting. Gradie grinned slowly as he remembered that incident. The weight of the women's thinking had forced the saloon owner to have the objectionable parts of the bull painted out, though even after two new coats of paint, they were still discernible. Human nature was a funny thing, Gradie thought. All of those women had seen dozens of bulls in the street, for Abilene was a trail town even before the railroad reached here. But a true painting of the animal was somehow shameful.

Gradie paused. Klimbaugh's restaurant was across the street. Gradie couldn't say he was really hungry. "Hell," he said in disgust. He knew what he was doing. He sought another excuse to delay riding out to the Huston place.

Arnold's grocery store was right ahead of him. Gradie did want something to put into his belly. Besides this would be a final, conclusive proof of the change in his appearance. He had known old man Arnold for as long as he could remember.

As he entered the store, its clutter struck him with force. He always remembered Tate Arnold as an orderly man, almost fussy in keeping his store neat. It wasn't that way any more. The store looked as though it hadn't been swept in weeks. The whole place had an air of neglect.

An old man tottered out from a rear room, and Gradie saw the reason for the noticeable change in the store's condition. This was Tate Arnold all right, but there was a sad and drastic change in him. He was no more than a shadow of the man Gradie remembered, and his encroaching feebleness showed in every step. Old age had caught up with Arnold. He could no longer do the things required to keep his store in its former shape. Gradie wondered why Arnold didn't just let go of the business, and another thought quickly changed his thinking. Maybe Arnold couldn't retire, maybe he needed the living this store brought him.

Arnold peered at Gradie through steel-rimmed glasses. "Don't I know you?" His voice wasn't firm, either.

"I don't know. Should you?" Gradie answered.

He suffered Arnold's scrutiny. This wasn't much of a test, not with Arnold's fading eyesight.

"Guess I don't," Arnold muttered. "Though it seems I ought to. What can I do for you?"

7

"A dime's worth of rattrap cheese and a nickel's worth of crackers."

"Sure," Arnold replied. He shuffled to the far end of the counter and flipped off the flynet from a large wheel of cheese. Either it was a new wheel, or not too many people were buying cheese.

It was a relatively new wheel, for the cheese cut without too much crumbling. Arnold sacked Gradie's crackers, tore off a piece of paper and wrapped the cheese. "Anything else?"

"That'll do," Gradie responded. He looked back from the door. Arnold still stared after him. Arnold was flogging a reluctant memory to tell him who this was.

# CHAPTER TWO

Gradie stopped outside the livery stable. He was still trying to fool himself, making every excuse he could to keep from starting out to his father's place. But dammit, he had to eat, didn't he? A mocking, inner voice said, "You could eat while you're riding."

He stubbornly shook his head at the tormenting inner voice. The water trough was under the shade of a tree. It looked like a more pleasant place to eat than in his saddle.

He walked over, sat down on the edge of the trough, and unwrapped his purchases. The cheese wasn't as fresh as it looked, but it would do. The crackers weren't too stale.

An eager whine diverted his attention. He would never look at a more disreputable dog. A dozen breeds had gone into making this one, and every part seemed completely mismatched. Its nose was as long as a wolf's, the head as broad as a mastiff's. It was almost as big as a wolf, and its hair was scruffy. Bristly whiskers covered its muzzle. The eyes got to Gradie. They were soft and pleading. By the looks of the thin rail of the backbone and the prominent ribs, this dog hadn't eaten for quite a while.

The dog whined again. It wanted to edge closer to Gradie, but sorry experience had taught the animal not to be brash enough to presume. Gradie suspected a lot of kicks had gone into that experience.

There were two kinds of hunger in the dog's eyes; hunger of the belly and hunger of the spirit.

"Poor critter," Gradie muttered. He held out his hand and snapped his fingers. "Come here. Come on, boy."

The dog quivered with eagerness, whipping its rear end back

and forth, but didn't move a fraction closer. He had learned some hard lessons well.

Gradie broke off a chunk of the cheese and held it out. How the dog wanted it. Its whining never ceased, and it drooled at the muzzle. Some leash of unseen cruelty held it rooted a safe distance away.

"Did somebody trick you, boy, then kick the hell out of you?" Gradie asked. He wouldn't be surprised. He had seen some unbelievable acts of cruelty to animals.

Gradie tossed the chunk of cheese toward the dog. It snapped at the cheese while it was in midair and missed. It buried its muzzle into the dust and gulped. The cheese disappeared, gone so fast that Gradie didn't see how the dog could taste the cheese.

He broke off more portions, making each toss shorter and shorter, inducing the animal to come closer to him. When he finally touched the dog, it went crazy with joy. It leaped repeatedly on him, trying to lick Gradie's face.

Gradie pushed it down with a firm hand. "Damn it, dog. I don't want you slobbering all over my face."

He fed the dog the last crumbs of the cheese, then handed him a cracker. Gradie thought soberly, companionship was one of the biggest needs in this sorry, old world.

After the dog consumed the last cracker, Gradie stood up. He still didn't want to go out to the Huston place. Was it fear of seeing his father and older brother again? He scoffed at the notion. He had grown past the stage where he had any fear of them left. He sighed heavily, no longer attempting to fool himself. It was that silent accusation in Hannah's eyes that he wanted to avoid.

The dog's whimpering demanded Gradie's attention. "Don't tell me you're still hungry, dog. All that cheese and crackers ought to put a pretty-good sized lump even in that belly of yours."

He reached down and ran his hand across the shaggy head. About a year, or a year and a half old, he thought. Probably nobody had ever cared enough about the animal to even give it a name.

"No name," he said aloud. "That's a damned shame. How does Dog sound to you?"

It seemed to suit Dog just fine, for he shook all over with delight at being spoke to.

"Dog, it is," Gradie said. "I'm going to get me a drink before I ride out of town."

He grinned ruefully as he thought, if Dog hung around him very long, he would do a lot of talking to him. It was sort of comforting at that to talk to Dog. He didn't have to watch every word to see that he didn't step on somebody's toes.

"One drink, Dog. That's all. I'm not a hard-drinking man." Lord knew he had seen his father and older brother drink themselves into sodden unconsciousness too many times. That had hurt all the Hustons, for when money was spent on whiskey, it was diverted from eating money. He patted Dog again. "But I need a drink this morning."

Dog's tail thumped against the ground. He looked like he understood. If he did, he didn't blame Gradie at all.

The Bull Head was the closest saloon, and Gradie walked to it. Dog never left his heels. Gradie hadn't claimed Dog, but Dog had done some claiming of his own.

At this time of the morning, the Bull Head was doing a poor business. Only one customer leaned against the bar, talking to the bartender.

Gradie's eyes adjusted to the shadowy interior, and he stopped short. He had only a side view of the customer, but he would never forget that square blocky shape. The short, thick neck made it look as though the head set squarely on the shoulders. Gradie's breathing whistled through his nostrils. He was tempted to back out hastily before Brad Cummings looked around and saw him. He cursed himself. All his running-away days were behind him.

Dog followed him into the saloon, slipping easily under the swinging doors. Gradie couldn't have kept him out, even if he had wanted to. He thought about it a moment, then shrugged. He was going to be in here only long enough to get a drink down. The bartender shouldn't raise too much hell about Dog being in here for that short a time.

Gradie put half of the long bar between himself and the lone customer. The cold block of his face looked as though it had been chisled out with an ice pick. Seeing Brad Cummings had opened another door in his mind. He had kept that door carefully closed, not wanting to see what it held again. The last time he had seen Cummings, Cummings had been kicking his ass half the length of Texas Street. Gradie had been on the scrawny side then, and only fourteen years old. He didn't have the heft, or the power, to stop Cummings from doing whatever he felt like doing. That old scene flashed before Gradie's eyes almost as vividly as though he was looking at it now.

The Cummingses' buckboard was out in front of Arnold's store, and Letty Cummings was coming out of the door. Her arms were laden with packages, and she struggled to reach the buckboard.

Gradie's heart picked up that familiar runaway pace. She was twelve years old with hair the color of a ripened field of wheat. Her eyes were the bluest Gradie had ever seen. He saw her every day at school, but he rarely talked to her, for his tongue always froze on him. But now she needed help and he sprang toward her.

"Let me carry them out to the buckboard," he mumbled as he reached out for the packages. He dared to look at her. She was willing; she appreciated his offer. She willingly changed the packages to Gradie's arms.

He had no idea where Brad Cummings came from. Gradie was certain Cummings hadn't been in sight when he first approached Letty.

Gradie was nearly to the buckboard when Cummings roared at him, "You damned ragpicker. I don't want you even talking to my daughter."

His first kick came then, propelling Gradie into the vehicle. His arms flew open, throwing packages in all directions.

"Papa," Letty screamed. "He's trying to help me."

Cummings's face was furious as he looked at her. "If you don't know who you are, I'll have to spend some time teaching you. No daughter of mine even speaks to trash like this."

Letty's face was white as she cast an imploring look at her father, but she didn't dare speak. She was afraid of him, and it showed.

Gradie scrambled to his feet. His back hurt. He couldn't stop the tears of pain and humiliation streaking his face. He had been kicked like a dog and before her.

"Damn you," he choked and ran at Cummings. He cut loose a wild swing that Cummings easily blocked. Cummings caught his arm and whirled him around. He kicked Gradie again. Those kicks hurt. The pain ran down into both legs. Gradie limped badly after the second one.

He was still hotheaded enough to attempt another run at Cummings. Cummings turned him and again rattled his teeth with another jolting kick.

Cummings's red, beefy face was filled with savage satisfaction. "Learn hard, don't you? If that's not enough, I'll be happy to oblige you."

A little sanity returned to Gradie's mind. He didn't have the size to stop Cummings from handling him this way. He cried openly now, his rage and humiliation tearing down any ordinary barrier to his tears. He didn't care who saw him. The smartest thing he could do was to get away from Cummings as fast as he could. Cummings would enjoy standing here and kicking him all day.

There hadn't been anybody out here when Cummings first kicked him. Now, there were more than a dozen, lining the walk, and more streamed this way. Gradie didn't see a kind face among them. All of them laughed with uproarious appreciation.

He wanted to get away from here as fast as he could, but those kicks had hurt him badly. He tried to run and bit his lower lip from the agony that washed through him. The best he could do was to limp away.

His humiliation wouldn't let him look at Letty. But hatred blazed out of his eyes before he turned away from Cummings.

"Why, you little bastard," Cummings roared. "Nobody looks at me like that, particularly your kind."

He followed and kicked Gradie again. Gradie wanted to yell

against the accumulation of the pain, but he kept his teeth clenched so that no sound would slip out. He tried to lengthen his stride and couldn't.

Cummings stayed right behind him. Every half-dozen steps or so, he kicked Gradie again. Gradie felt he had been kicked the length of Texas Street, before Cummings tired of his fun and turned back.

Tears dimmed Gradie's vision, but not so much that he couldn't see the people flock about Cummings and slap him on the back. Cummings was the richest man in the county. He owned half of it, and people were careful to keep in his good graces.

The sobbing tore Gradie apart. Oh, goddam him. He repeated it with every limping step. How he wished he had a gun; he would kill Cummings right now. Deep down, he knew he would never do anything. Thinking about revenge was all the luxury his class could afford.

The scene slowly faded. Gradie hadn't thought of it often. He hadn't allowed himself to think of it. Occasionally, he had vowed he would return some day and pay back the humiliation and hurt. But time had a way of blunting humiliation. He would never have a better opportunity than now, but it no longer mattered that much.

"Bartender," he said. His voice was normal. "I want a whiskey."

Cummings was in the midst of telling something to the bartender, and the bartender listened attentively.

Cummings flung an annoyed glance at Gradie, but he made no comment. Gradie wondered sardonically if time had also mellowed Cummings some.

"Take care of him," Cummings growled.

He watched Gradie in the back mirror, but showed no real interest. Evidently, Cummings hadn't recognized Gradie.

The bartender had never known Gradie. He poured Gradie a drink, pocketed the proffered coin, his impatience plain to see. He wanted to get back to Cummings's story.

One thing certainly hasn't changed, Gradie thought wryly. Cummings is still Mr. Big around here. People make sure they don't offend him.

He studied Cummings in the back mirror as he sipped his drink. Cummings must still be puzzled, for every now and then, his glance strayed to Gradie's reflection. Six years had made a noticeable change in Cummings. His paunch now hung over his belt, and his jowls had thickened. His face was lined and sagging, and gray streaked his hair. Gradie couldn't help hoping that age was riding Cummings as cruelly as it seemed to be.

Gradie finished his glass and set it down on the bar. Dog had been sniffing all over the place. Now, he approached Cummings and sniffed at his boots.

Cummings turned from the bar, his face flushing in sudden rage. "Get away from me, you damned cur," he yelled. He aimed a kick at Dog, but Dog was adroit from the practice of having avoided many kicks. He jumped nimbly to one side, and his teeth bared in a snarl.

"Come over here, Dog," Gradie ordered. "Bite him, and he'll poison you."

A brick-red flooded Cummings's face, and momentarily, he was speechless as he struggled to regain his breath the surprise had knocked out of him.

"Who the hell do you think you are, talking to me like that?" he roared.

"Don't you know?" Gradie jeered. "You're old and fat, Brad. You're not as good a kicker as you once were."

Color fled Cummings's face, leaving it strained and gray. He had puzzled over the identity of this stranger ever since he came in, but he still couldn't put a name to him.

"Who are you?" he growled.

"Does it matter?" Gradie asked mockingly. "Your kind doesn't associate with my kind."

Comprehension dawned in Cummings's eyes. "You're that snot-nosed Huston kid, the one I had to kick his ass to learn him something."

All the jeering and mockery vanished from Gradie's voice. It was flint-hard now and as cold as a January day. "Would you like to try it now, Cummings?"

Cummings took a step toward Gradie, trying to regain some of his former bluster. He stabbed a finger at Gradie, but his roar lacked its former volume. "Hear this. You stay away from Letty. If I catch you anywhere near her—" The words faded away uncertainly. Those gray eyes never veered. Cummings felt as though they reached clear to his backbone and riveted there.

"You'll what?" Gradie said.

Cummings looked blackly at him and said, "You'll see."

Gradie could have told him that his former interest in Letty Cummings was a schoolboy fascination, that he had no interest of any kind in any of the Cummingses. He withheld the words, not wanting to give Cummings that much consolation. Let him sweat a little.

"Come on, Dog," he said and started for the door.

Dog still circled Cummings, his fangs showing.

Gradie stopped at the door. "Dog, did you hear me?"

Dog heard him. He whirled, ran toward Gradie, and leaped upon him. Gradie caught him and carried him out of the saloon. The last thing he saw of Cummings and the bartender was their heads close together. Now, all of Abilene would know that Gradie Huston was back. It didn't matter a damned bit. He wasn't going to stay here long enough for Abilene to mouth his return very much.

# CHAPTER THREE

Dog followed Gradie to the livery stable. Gradie stepped inside the runway, and Sawyer bounded out of his chair. Good service didn't motivate him. He wanted to keep that mongrel from entering.

"Get," he shouted, waving his arms. "Beat it." He was a scrawny man with a mean, pinched face. Gradie would place him somewhere in his fifties.

Dog retreated a wary yard. Those liquid eyes begged Gradie for help.

"Let him alone," Gradie ordered. "Who does he belong to?"

The hostler snorted. "Have you taken a good look at him? Who would have him?"

"I would," Gradie said levelly. He knew the feeling of being lonesome, of not being wanted.

Sawyer gave Gradie a queer look, shook his head, and muttered, "Do you want your horse?"

"That's what I'm here for." Gradie grinned at Sawyer's retreating back. This was no way to set out making himself popular with the people of Abilene, but he wasn't going to be around long enough to make any difference.

He whistled Dog over to him, put his hand on his head, and pressed him into a sitting position. "Hold it," he said.

Dog's tail thumped the ground as Gradie stroked his head. Dog wasn't anything for looks, but he obeyed pretty well, and he picked up things fast.

"You got a brain in that ugly head?" Gradie asked.

The tail thumped harder, raising a small cloud of dust.

Sawyer came back with Eagle. Eagle was a gelding, but he

still had a spark of meanness in him. He had dumped Gradie several times, particularly when the morning was frosty. Gradie imagined that Eagle would be a handful of hell, if he had been left a stallion.

Dog ran up to the gelding, and Gradie amost yelled at him. He cut it short. Dog could get his head kicked off, but if he was going to be around Eagle very much, he might as well learn how much Eagle would take.

Eagle thrust his muzzle down against Dog's nose, then snorted and jerked his head up. Gradie watched closely. Maybe Dog didn't smell good. That was entirely possible.

Dog stood his ground. He whined deep in his throat, and it sounded as though he begged for understanding. Eagle put his head back down again, and their noses touched. Dog's rough tongue licked Eagle across the muzzle.

It surprised Gradie that Eagle didn't at least jerk his head up. Eagle had exploded before for far lesser matters. Instead, Eagle whinnied, and Dog whined. Damned if it didn't sound as though those two were trying to converse with each other. Gradie shook his head. Animals were kinder than most people. A rough or unattractive exterior didn't seem to bother them, or turn them away.

Sawyer swore softly. "Damned if it don't look like they're making up. Looks like you've got a dumb horse, or else he's blind, mister."

"Or a lot smarter than most people," Gradie said drily.

It took a moment for Sawyer to get Gradie's meaning, then he flushed. "Shit," he said furiously.

Gradie grinned and swung up. He headed Eagle out onto the street. He looked behind him only once. Dog trotted right behind the horse. The Huston soddy was a full two miles out of town. Eagle could run away and leave Dog before a quarter of that distance was covered. Gradie kept Eagle down to a slow pace. He wouldn't say it was because of kindheartedness toward Dog, just a reluctance to get out there. What would he say when he saw his ma. A half-dozen greetings ran through his mind, and he discarded all of them. What would fit the occasion? He guessed he would just say "Hello, Ma" and see what happened from there on.

He stopped short when he came in sight of the soddy. It looked worse than he remembered, but then a kid wasn't as aware of abuse and neglect as a grownup was. The soddy had a tired, sagging look, and Gradie wondered how much longer it would stand. Without inspecting the roof, he would bet it leaked. Weeds grew up chest-high all around it, and a pile of tin cans rose higher than the weeds. A few well-used paths had kept the weeds under a semblance of control, but the rest of the yard was a jungle.

Gradie's lips twisted in disgust, as he looked slowly about him. He had almost forgotten that people could live this poorly. A wagon had broken down in the front yard, and no effort had been made to remove, or repair it. It had set there, rotting in the summer sun and winter snow. Now, it was beyond repair. The whole yard was filled with litter. No effort had been made to pick any of it up, or to put anything away.

"Goddammit," Gradie said helplessly. How could people stand to live like this?

That familiar sense of helplessness seized him, and he wanted to turn and flee. It was a familiar feeling. He had felt it strongly the day he left Abilene.

He swung down and led Eagle through the weeds to within a few yards of the door. He knew what it would look like without stepping inside.

A thin spiral of smoke rose from the length of stovepipe extending through the roof. Somebody was home. Gradie's mouth was suddenly dry, and he didn't think he was going to be able to speak.

He swallowed hard, then said hoarsely, "Anybody home?"

A woman came to the doorway. She peered uncertainly at Gradie, then said falteringly, "Is it you, Gradie?"

She had aged horribly and was much thinner than Gradie remembered. He didn't recall all the gray in her hair, either. He remembered how beautiful that glossy black hair had been. All the life was gone from it, and while she had tried to gather it up in a bun at the back of her neck, wisps of it straggled over her face.

"Gradie?" she repeated.

It was hard to speak over the big lump that had suddenly blocked his throat. "It's me, Ma. Gradie."

He thought her face was going to break up into small pieces. He opened his arms, and she rushed into them. Her sobbing racked her body. My God, how frail she was.

Gradie let her cry, helpless to know what to say or do to comfort her.

She lifted her head and knuckled at the tears in her eyes. "I'm foolish," she said flatly. The catch in her voice appeared again. "But it's been so long. I dreamed that some day you'd—" She was unable to continue for a moment.

"I know," he said. His mind was a huge void, and he was unable to think of anything to fill it. Maybe stopping by here hadn't been such a good idea.

She shook her head half angrily and used the hem of her skirt to dry her eyes. "You're looking just fine, Gradie."

His guilt flogged him, and he had to say something to ease his conscience. "Ma, I didn't want to go." He was aware of the pleading note in his voice. "I tried to get you to go with me."

A ghost of a smile moved her lips, and she touched his face with a finger. "Things just got too bad for you to stand, Gradie. You had to go. I remember how you begged me, but I couldn't."

"You could go now, Ma."

She shook her head, a slow, sad movement, but the motion said it all.

"You're still in love with Jude," he accused angrily.

Her face was thoughtful as though she was just reaching a conclusion. "I haven't been in love with your pa for years, Gradie. Don't be blaming yourself. Things just turned out that way."

Gradie knew a complete sense of defeat. They faced the same old impasse. Nothing ever changed.

She broke the strain of the moment by raising her voice and calling, "Jonse, come out and see who's here."

Gradie winced as he heard the familiar, dragging step. That hadn't changed, either.

Jonse came to the door and asked, "Who is it, Ma?"

Jonse was far worse than Gradie remembered. He slurred his words until they were hard to understand. His face was too thin, his body wasted. If anything, Jonse seemed even smaller than when Gradie left home. Those eyes were too bright, Gradie thought. He had seen fever-induced brightness before. Now, he understood his mother's repeated refusal to leave. Jonse was worse.

"Don't you remember me, Jonse?" he asked softly.

Jonse's face crumbled, and he looked as though he was going to cry. "It's Gradie, ain't it?" he asked uncertainly.

"You know it is," Gradie replied.

He jumped forward to prevent Jonse from taking any more steps than he had to. Jonse could only wrap one arm about him. He didn't handle the withered arm nearly as well as Gradie recalled.

Gradie raged inwardly. Jonse had had a hell of a life, and there weren't any better prospects ahead of him.

"You're not going to leave us again, are you?" Jonse asked.

Gradie lied to those begging eyes. "No, Jonse. I'm not going to leave you again."

Dog couldn't stand being left out of things any longer. He leaped up on the two of them, his weight making Jonse stagger.

"Get down, damn it," Gradie swore.

Jonse wrapped his good arm around Dog's neck. His laugh bubbled with delight as Dog licked his face. "Your dog, Gradie? I never had a dog."

Gradie almost said, "He's yours" and bit down on the words. He doubted that Dog could last very long around here. Either Jude or Phil would run him off, or shoot him.

"We'll see, Jonse," he temporized.

"Is he hungry?"

"I imagine; he always is," Gradie said drily.

"What can I feed him?"

Gradie grinned. "He'll eat anything that won't eat him." His eyes questioned Hannah.

That lost, futile look was in her eyes again. "I haven't a thing, Gradie. Unless it's a can of bacon grease. Would he eat that?"

"He sure would," Gradie said promptly.

Hannah turned toward the house. "I'll get it." Jonse was too absorbed in the dog to even look up.

Hannah came back with a can of congealed grease and a spoon. She spooned out great gobs of the unsavory-looking stuff and dropped them on the ground. Dog gobbled them up before they hardly hit the ground.

With each gulp, Jonse chortled with delight. Gradie's throat hurt as he watched the scene. He looked at Hannah's face, and it was suffused with love and devotion. Gradie would never have to ask another question about why she stayed here.

He turned his head as the dismal creaking of an ungreased axle squealed in torture against a dry hub. He had been here only a few minutes, but that was too long. The dilapidated buggy, holding Jude and Phil was coming down the road.

Gradie watched the buggy with a critical eye. With each rotation one of the wheels wobbled, and the rim looked as though it would come off at any second. If his father or brother didn't do something about that wheel, they were going to be afoot and soon.

Hannah's face was strained and fearful. She had known too many ugly, physical scenes between the two in the buggy and Gradie. Even Jonse's easy outgoing manner had vanished. He sat with his good arm around the dog, his eyes apprehensive.

Gradie's face was an inscrutable mask as he watched Jude pull up the tired, old ancient horse. Gradie's eyes burned as he looked at the skinny ribs of the animal. Nothing could restore the horse's vanished vitality, but a few decent meals would help.

Jude squinted at Gradie uncertainly. He was a heavy man, almost gross, and his face was puffy and red. Gradie doubted that a razor or washcloth had touched Jude's face in a month. Jude climbed down, moving as though his feet hurt him. The tails of a dirty shirt hung out over his overalls.

"Hell, don't you know him, Pa?" Phil drawled. He was an

exact replica of his father. He had already caught up with Jude in weight, and it wouldn't be long before he passed him.

Gradie hated both of them with an intensity that almost made him ill. Those two pairs of meaty hands had knocked him around, never waiting for a real reason, except the mean satisfaction hurting somebody else gave them. Gradie felt weak with the waves of hatred. You shouldn't have come back, he kept repeating to himself. Nothing ever changed.

Gradie got a firm grip on himself. He hadn't matured as much as he supposed. He still looked at this pair through the eyes of a child. He forced the passion out of his eyes, knowing he was far beyond their reach. They couldn't touch him again. In place of the hatred, he felt only disgust. No wonder Cummings referred to all of the Hustons as trash.

Phil was pleased with himself in seeing something his father couldn't see. "Don't you recognize him, Pa? How can you forget that ugly face? I'd know it anyplace. That's my middle brother."

He climbed down from the buggy and approached Gradie. His ponderous weight made him roll as he walked.

"So my runaway brother decided to come home." His eyes ran over Gradie, taking him in from head to toe. He didn't miss a thing, the good hat, the almost new boots.

"Looks like he's done all right for hisself," Phil muttered. The envy was plain in his face. "Yes, sir. Done all right. I wouldn't mind having a shirt like that." He reached out to finger the material.

Gradie struck the hand aside. "Keep your hand off me," he warned.

He heard Hannah's little squeal of terror but didn't look around. She was familiar with such scenes, and it put a dread in her.

Phil's mouth sagged open. He looked at his forearm that Gradie struck, then roared, "You sure ain't got any smarter. All them lessons I taught you don't seem to have stuck."

He thrust his angry face forward and came toward Gradie with heavy, purposeful strides. Both of those meaty fists were bunched. Gradie remembered that once the sight of those ready fists would have filled him with terror. It didn't now. He evaluated the situation carefully. Phil outweighed him by many pounds, but he was slow and clumsy. Gradie welcomed the coming encounter. He had a long bill to collect.

Phil was too engrossed in anticipation of hitting Gradie again to see Dog spring at him. Gradie did. Dog's fangs were bared, and his eyes were baleful. Gradie grinned at a thought that hit him. It looked as though nobody laid a hand on Gradie while Dog was around. Gradie supposed he could call Dog off, but it would give him a wicked satisfaction to see Dog take a chunk out of Phil's leg.

Dog sank his teeth in Phil's calf. Stunned surprise washed Phil's face before he howled in pain. He hopped around on one leg, kicking with the other, trying to shake Dog loose. Among those mixed ancestors Gradie was sure was in Dog, one of them had to be bulldog, for Dog clung so tenaciously.

Gradie thoroughly enjoyed watching this. Dog was doing some damage, for streaks of red stained Phil's overall leg. Gradie wouldn't have believed that Phil could have covered so much space on one leg as he thrashed about trying to dislodge the dog.

Dog finally let go and retreated a cautious distance, his snarl still fixed, the eyes yellow and baleful.

Phil looked at his leg. His overalls were ripped below his knee. "Look what he did to me," he bawled. "I'll kill him. I'll knock his goddam head off."

He spied a scantling, partially hidden in the weeds. Phil bellowed with triumph as he sprang toward it. He picked it up and swung it around his head, making it whistle. "Where's that damned dog?" he demanded.

Dog was almost belly down to the ground as he slunk about the perimeter of the circle in which Phil stood. The scantling didn't scare him at all. He had been threatened too often with all sorts of sticks and clubs.

"That's enough, Dog," Gradie snapped. He would swear Dog looked puzzled. Gradie kept his face straight. Here Dog had sprung to his aid, and he was being called off. No wonder humans were so difficult to understand.

Dog didn't move, but his snarling never ceased.

Phil started toward him, his face mean, the scantling cocked over his shoulder.

"Drop that board, Phil," Gradie commanded.

Phil swung ugly eyes toward him. "I'd just as soon knock your head off."

"You've got more brains than to try it," Gradie said calmly.

"I'll show you," Phil howled and ran at him.

Gradie was surprised that Dog didn't try to take Phil again. Gradie's order to Dog held him motionless. That kind of obedience made him feel good. He kept a careful eye on the scantling in Phil's hands. How would Phil use it? Would he jab at him with one end, or would he swing it like a club, trying to rip off Gradie's head?

Phil planted himself a couple of feet from Gradie and whipped the scantling around. Gradie ducked, letting the board whistle over his head.

He stepped in close and tried to drive his fist through Phil's belly. He buried the fist wrist-deep in the soft flesh. The breath whooshed out of Phil's lungs. His eyes rolled in his head, and his face turned a definite greenish cast. He dropped the scantling and wrapped both arms around his outraged belly. He sank slowly to the ground. Gradie thought he was going to be sick.

"You can't hit Phil like that," Jude yelled. He didn't make the mistake of trying to get close to Gradie.

That tight grin was back on Gradie's lips. "You show me another way, Pa, and I'll hit him your way."

Phil still couldn't talk. His mouth was open, but a piteous moan was the only sound coming from it.

Gradie looked at Hannah. "I'm sorry, Ma." The apology was not for hitting Phil, he would gladly do that over again. He was sorry for the way his short visit turned out. Jude and Phil might take out their spite on her.

"I'll be back, Ma," he said softly.

"You promise?" Her eyes were more eloquent than her words.

"I promise," he answered.

Gradie mounted and whistled to Dog. He doubted that he needed to; Dog would go anyplace Gradie went.

Jonse's face was all wrinkled up with distress. "You're taking my dog," he wailed.

Phil hadn't yet got up. He still nursed his tender belly, but his face was slowly returning to normal color.

Gradie wished he could explain to Jonse that Dog wouldn't last long, if Gradie left him behind. The first thing Phil would do when he was able, would be to get his hands on a gun and shoot Dog.

"I'll bring him back, Jonse."

Some of the distress eased off Jonse's face.

"You promise?" he asked dubiously.

That was two who asked the same question. How could Gradie fail either of them?

# CHAPTER FOUR

Brad Cummings was in a foul mood as he approached his house. What in the hell was that no-good Gradie Huston doing back? Cummings had fretted over that unanswered question all the way home. Did Gradie intend to stay? That was the question that bothered Cummings the most. Another twin question that disturbed him almost as much, was how would Letty react to the news that Gradie had returned?

Six years ago, Letty had been interested in Gradie. Cummings remembered well how brokenhearted she had been after he kicked Gradie's ass down Texas Street. She was even worse after Gradie left. For a solid month she refused to speak to her father, blaming him for making Gradie leave.

Cummings swore and shook his head. There was no use fretting over something that had happened that far back. Letty was grown up now, and Cummings thought she would have forgotten his treatment of Gradie long ago. But at times, he wasn't so sure. Though she never spoke of it, she would look at him with the hostility thinly veiled in her eyes. At those times, Cummings couldn't help feeling she would never forgive him. He wouldn't tell her about seeing Gradie this morning, and he hoped nobody else would.

He sighed heavily, feeling the old despondency returning. It was pure hell raising a daughter without a wife to help him out. Molly had died when Letty was only two years old. The Lord knew that Cummings had done everything possible to raise Letty properly. She always had the best money could buy, and he tried to give her whatever she wanted, if he thought it was good for her. He had constantly tried to impress upon her that she was

Letty Cummings, a far cut above anybody else in this community. He never seemed to be quite able to drive that point home. She was overly friendly with everybody. Reasoning and raging did no good. She couldn't seem to get it through her head that she was a Cummings. She had time for everybody who came along, and she poured out her sympathy to anybody who asked for it. That thought made Cummings snort. She would have supported those worthless Hustons, if he hadn't stepped in and stopped her.

He rode around to the back of the house, and a scowl blackened his face. Ord Simmons, one of his riders, was talking to Letty. Simmons must have said something that amused Letty, for her peal of laughter rang out. It infuriated Cummings. Simmons seized every possible opportunity to talk to Letty. He was a good hand, but Cummings suspected he would have to fire him soon.

Letty looked up and saw her father. Her face sobered, and that chilling remoteness was in her eyes again. Cummings had seen her look like that before. It always left him uncomfortable and lonely.

Each day, she grew to look more like her mother. She had the fine cameo carved quality to her features. She had Molly's same warmth, though she rarely displayed any of it around her father. The sense of loss angered and saddened Cummings at the same time. He had gone over their relationship a thousand times, and he couldn't see where he was in the wrong.

Cummings rode up to them and swung down. He grunted as his boots touched the ground. Each year that damned rheumatism seemed to take a deeper bite.

He intended to remain calm, but his voice kept rising. "Goddammit, Ord. This all you got to do? I told you to—" Letty was listening, and Cummings chopped the sentence short. He didn't want her to know that he was having the Hustons watched. He was certain that Jude and Phil were killing and butchering an occasional head of his stock, but so far he hadn't been able to prove it. The loss of a few head wouldn't dent him, but goddammit, nobody touched anything that belonged to him. He didn't care how long it took to nail down those two thieves. For the past two weeks, he had two of his riders watching every move they made. One of these days, he would catch that trash in the actual deed, then he would be able to get rid of them for good.

He wasn't sure how Letty would react, if she heard what he was doing. He couldn't afford the risk of her refusing to talk to him for another long stretch. She could live in a secret part of her own mind that he couldn't touch at all.

"I've got some private business to talk over with Ord," he growled.

Letty stared at him. He couldn't read a thing in those fathomless eyes. When such moments of stress occurred, they were two strangers facing each other.

Without speaking, she turned and went into the house, her shoulders squared, her head carried high. Cummings groaned inwardly. She was offended again. He wished she could see that everything he did was for her good.

Simmons stirred uneasily. He had been around long enough to tread warily around the boss, particularly when he looked like this. Simmons wasn't much older than Letty and was handsome in a lean, rugged way.

Cummings glowered at him. He was very much aware of how Simmons's eyes lit up every time he saw Letty. Cummings was going to say something about that and soon.

"I thought I told you to watch the Hustons."

Simmons threw out a hand in helpless supplication. "That's what I was doing, boss. I was out with Pike. We followed the Hustons all morning. They were driving that old buggy." His eyes burned with the taste of success. "They got within fifty yards of a steer. Phil shot him from the buggy. That's what I rode in to tell you. Letty said she thought you'd be back from town soon."

"You didn't let them get away?" Cummings barked.

Simmons shook his head. "Pike's still watching them. Old man Wilkie joined Jude and Phil. He drove up in his wagon. They'll be there quite a time. They were just beginning to butcher when I left to get you."

Old man Wilkie was of the same ilk as the Hustons. Cummings

had never known him to put in much time working. So that
was how the Hustons got rid of an animal so slick. They butchered the steer on the spot, and Wilkie hauled it away. The three
probably had an outlet for their meat. Cummings didn't know
where that outlet was, but once the lid was jerked off, a lot of
things would come into view.

"Where are they?" Cummings asked heatedly.

"You know that big double bend on Pony Creek?" At Cummings's nod, Simmons went on, "Right beside the first bend. I
left Pike on the bluff overlooking it."

Cummings swore viciously. The damned Hustons were getting
bolder. They took time to butcher on Cummings's land.

"Go into town and tell Slaughter what's happening." He
grinned evilly. "I want to make this hanging legal."

"Do you want his deputies?"

"Sure," Cummings answered. "I want a lot of people to come
to this party."

Cummings walked back to his horse and mounted. He didn't
even think of his aching legs. He felt better this morning than
he had for a long time.

Simmons raced off in the direction of Abilene. Time wasn't too
precious now. If the Hustons and Wilkie finished their butchering
and drove off before Slaughter arrived, Wilkie's wagon could be
run down. That old wagon was in pretty sorry shape.

Cummings glanced at the house as he whirled his horse around.
Letty stood at a window, watching him. If she knew what was
happening, she would probably ask for leniency for those beef
thieves. That mean grin returned to Cummings's mouth. Well,
she wouldn't get it. He had only one regret about the whole
matter. Gradie Huston was back. Cummings wished he was one
of the three thieves instead of Old man Wilkie.

He spurred his horse hard, approaching the bluff from the back
side. He swore furiously as he saw Pike standing erect at the lip
of the bluff. What the hell was the fool doing; trying to give
those three thieves a warning to get away?

Pike had worked for Cummings many years. He was short and
wizened, permanently lamed from a bad fall. But he was still a

capable man on horseback. He was familiar with that look on Cummings's face. The boss was about ready to raise hell.

Pike held up his hand, checking Cummings's outburst. "They've gone, boss. Not over five minutes ago. The Hustons went that-away." He gestured to the east. "Old man Wilkie drove his wagon northwest." He squinted up at Cummings. "That old wagon didn't look like it could go very far. Do you think he's trying to reach Moonlight?"

That could be Wilkie's destination. Moonlight was less than five miles from this spot. Wilkie might have a customer in that small town for freshly butchered beef.

Cummings's black study worried Pike. He was afraid he was the source of it. "Hell, we can overtake Wilkie before he gets there. We—"

Cummings cut him short with an impatient slash of his hand. "I'm not concerned about catching him. We're waiting until Slaughter gets here. Ord went after him."

He seethed as he glared at the bend of the creek. Even from here he could see where the grass had been trampled down.

He looked at Pike. "Is that where they butchered?" Maybe it was a good thing he hadn't arrived while the butchering was going on. He doubted that he could contain his temper and not shoot them.

Pike nodded. "Dropped the steer right there. Phil did the shooting. Picked a comfortable place to work, didn't they? They had good shade."

"They won't be working much longer at anything," Cummings said in a bleak voice. He rode down a steep incline, not waiting for Pike to join him. He didn't look around as he heard Pike following him.

Cummings stopped at the trampled grass and thought he would burst with rage. The ground was soaked with blood, and the smell of blood was in the air. The intestines and offal were discarded near the creek, and flies swarmed over them, so numerous that they turned the intestines and offal black. The flies buzzed angrily as they rose at Cummings's approach, then settled back when Cummings halted.

Pike had been looking around. "They didn't leave the hide," he said.

Cummings could understand that. Leaving a branded hide around would be a voice yelling that this was where the rustling occurred. No, the hide was probably in Wilkie's wagon, carried away to be disposed of safely later. By morning, all other remains would be gone. Predators of all species would be drawn to this spot before this day was out, and they would effectively gobble up all accusing traces.

Cummings couldn't sit still while he waited for Slaughter and Simmons. He got down and moved restlessly about, his steps jerky and abrupt. My God, what was taking Slaughter so long? Already, he must have waited more than a half-hour.

He realized it couldn't have been that long. When he dismounted, his attention was drawn to the shadow of a tree trunk over a rock. The shadow had barely moved. Cummings tried to contain himself. Slaughter would get here as fast as he could. He wouldn't dare to defy Cummings's order.

The waiting made Pike jittery, and he suggested, "Brad, we could go after Wilkie anytime you're ready. He's got the proof in his wagon. I saw him and the Hustons load the meat in the wagon. What more proof do we need?"

His words faltered before the coldly critical eyes fixed on him. "Did you have some idea of taking them up before a judge?"

"Something like that," Pike said meekly.

"If a judge listened to your proof, what would he give them?" Cummings demanded caustically. "Maybe five years. That's not enough. I want this country rid of scum like them, rid permanently."

Cummings turned to resume his pacing. Pike shivered. There was one vindictive man. Pike didn't know of anybody who successfully crossed Brad Cummings.

Pike sat down on a rock. That lame leg was beginning to act up on him again. He wanted to know how long Cummings intended to wait, but he didn't dare ask. His nerves were buckling under the strain. He had rolled and smoked one cigarette after another. A half-dozen butts lay around his feet. He was opening the tobacco sack to roll another cigarette when he heard distant hoofbeats.

He lifted his head and listened. Several horses were headed this way at a hard gallop.

"Horses coming," he announced to Cummings.

"You think I'm deaf?" Cummings snarled.

Relief eased some of the tension in Cummings's face as three horsemen came into view. He had been afraid Simmons hadn't been able to find Slaughter.

Cummings showed no friendliness as Dent Slaughter and his deputy, Hebb Inman, pulled to a stop before him. He had backed Slaughter in the last election, and now, he was certain he had made a mistake. Slaughter was all bluster with nothing inside to back up the bluster. By God, Cummings could correct that mistake. The next election was only a month away.

Slaughter was a short, blocky man with a florid face. He was never able to look Cummings straight in the eye. "Ord told me about the butchering, Brad. But I sure don't see anything around here."

Hebb Inman, Slaughter's deputy had sharper eyes, or was more alert. He was a full head taller than Slaughter, and his deputy badge gave him the authority he needed to back up his usual aggressive manner. His face looked like a piece of metal that had been hammered out on an anvil. He thought that every woman in Abilene sharpened their eyes when he walked by. Cummings had no use for Inman, either. He hadn't missed the attention Inman tried to pay Letty whenever he could.

Neither of them was worth a damn, he thought. They both worked at being popular instead of doing their job. Cummings got a savage pleasure in thinking that the next election would get rid of both of them.

Inman pointed at the blood-soaked ground, and the intestines and offal. "Looks like some butchering's been done there, Dent."

Slaughter's face burned. It always burned whenever Inman tried to show him up. "I just saw it," he said testily.

He looked at Cummings's stony face. Cummings hadn't missed

that exchange between Slaughter and Inman. The old bastard would file it away in his head and use it when he could hurt Slaughter the most.

"I can't take a handful of bloody ground into court as proof." Slaughter said. That should cut Cummings down.

Cummings looked at him with contempt. He stared at Slaughter a long moment. Slaughter withered under the full impact of those merciless eyes.

"I'd expect you to say something like that." Cummings growled. "Even enough proof for you is in a wagon not over a couple of miles from here. Keep your mouth shut and don't make a bigger fool of yourself until we get there."

Slaughter could feel the heat burning in his face. He looked at Inman. Inman's expression was blank, but Slaughter knew he was gloating inside.

# CHAPTER FIVE

Old man Wilkie didn't know horsemen were anywhere near him until they surrounded his wagon. He had been semi-dozing in the increasing heat of the morning's sun; when he looked up, there they were, on both sides of his wagon.

Wilkie presented a disreputable appearance. The crown of his hat was broken, and gray locks of hair stuck out in several places. He was filthy dirty, and the accumulated grime was packed in the age lines of his face. Nobody had ever known Wilkie to do any work. He lived a long time without that necessity, for he was in his sixties.

Wilkie couldn't meet any of those hard, inquisitive eyes. He tried to say a bright, "Howdy," but his lips were dry and stiff, and the word came out a croaking rasp. His eyes flicked from the badges on Slaughter's and Inman's shirts, then to Cummings and his two riders. Cummings put more fear in him than all the others combined.

The five riders fell into pace with the wagon and rode several moments without saying anything. Sweat broke out on Wilkie's forehead and trickled down his face. He could feel the itching course of sweat from his armpits.

"Ord, we can't visit very well with the wagon going," Cummings said. "Maybe you'd better stop it."

Simmons rode up even with the tired, old mule, grabbed its bridle, and stopped the animal. The groaning creak of the wagon ceased, and the silence became oppressive.

They just sat and looked at the old man. Wilkie couldn't stand it any longer. He licked his lips before he could speak. "What the hell did you do that for?" He tried to yell the protest, but the words came out reedy and thin.

Cummings fixed him with a merciless stare. "Don't you know, Wilkie?" He shook his head. "Now, that's odd. I sure thought you would."

Wilkie's tongue clove to the roof of his mouth. He tried to think of something to say, and his mind was blank.

"What are you doing on my land?" Cummings asked with ominous softness.

Wilkie made a feeble gesture. "Shucks, Brad. I was just taking a shortcut. Didn't think you'd mind."

"Is that what's making you sweat so hard, Wilkie?" A cruel, little smile played on Cummings's mouth. "Or is it something you're carrying in the wagon?"

Fear was a hard knot, blocking Wilkie's throat. He had to try a couple of times before he could get out a few, squeaky words.

"Nothing in there, Brad. Nothing at all."

Cummings moved to the wagon bed and stared into it. "You've got something in here, Wilkie. You've got it covered with a tarpaulin."

Raw terror made Wilkie scream inwardly. He wasn't much of a praying man, but he prayed now. "Don't let him look under there, God," he said over and over.

Cummings played with him like a cat with a helpless mouse. "You're not carrying a body under that tarp, are you, Wilkie?" He leaned over from his saddle and ran his forefinger over the tarpaulin. He straightened and held up the stained finger for Wilkie to see. "Damned, if that doesn't look like blood to me. What do you think, Sheriff?"

Slaughter enjoyed the game, too. "Maybe we'd better take a look."

He leaned over, seized the tarpaulin, and stripped it from the chunks of beef. "Would you look at this, Brad. Looks like old Wilkie did some butchering this morning. He's got a hide in the wagon, too. Now why would he want to carry something like that around?"

"Pike! Ord! Spread it out," Cummings ordered.

A green hide was heavy, and Pike and Ord struggled to drag it out of the wagon and spread it hairside up on the ground.

The groan deep in Wilkie's throat sounded like an animal in mortal pain. The brand on the hide was almost as big as a dinner plate. The Circle C accused him louder than a thousand words.

"Didn't want to bury it on my land, did you, Wilkie," Cummings purred. "Afraid somebody might see all of that digging and wonder what was under all that dirt? Where did you plan to get rid of it? Does the same place you sell the meat buy hides too? If I ain't wrong, I believe that animal once belonged to me." He lifted his paw and let the mouse run a little way before he slapped the paw back down. "It's hard for me to believe that a scrawny, old man could have done the killing and all that butchering by himself."

"I didn't." Wilkie screamed. "I was just passing by, and they forced me to help load the meat." He shook as though in the midst of a seizure of high fever. "They forced me into it," he moaned. "You gotta believe me. I didn't want no part of it. They said they'd kill me, if I didn't help them."

"You better name them," Cummings said.

"Jude and Phil Huston," Wilkie babbled. "It was all their doing."

"You hear that, Sheriff?" Cummings asked. "You know Wilkie wouldn't lie."

Slaughter snorted, and Inman laughed. Pike and Simmons exchanged knowing grins.

Cummings stabbed a finger at Wilkie. "You're trying to tell us that the Hustons rode off and left all of this meat? You know you'd better think of a better story."

Wilkie's face was the color of a dead fish's belly, and he gasped for breath. His features were contorted as he frantically tried to come up with something that would take this relentless pressure off of him. "They didn't want to be caught with the meat on your land. They told me to drive the wagon off your land. They'd join me then." He pointed vaguely. "They're waiting for me out there someplace."

Cummings's face was as cold as the heart of a glacier. He was through playing with Wilkie. "You goddam liar," he raged. "You were in with them from the start. How many times have you done this before? Where are you selling the meat? In Moonlight?"

Wilkie's eyes were glazed, and he looked half out of his mind. If he heard Cummings's question, he didn't answer. "They made me," he whimpered.

"Pike," Cummings commanded. "Get down and drive that mule. In the shape Wilkie is in, there's no telling what he'd do."

Pike dismounted and tied his pony to the back of the wagon. He climbed up beside Wilkie and lifted the reins. He sniffed, and his nose wrinkled in disgust. He pushed Wilkie over on the seat. "You stink, old man. Stay away from me."

"Brad," he said, "where do you want me to go?"

"Use your head," Cummings snapped. "Take him over to the Hustons'. I want this over in a hurry."

He glared at Slaughter as though he was challenging Slaughter's opposition.

Slaughter wouldn't meet his eyes. "Guess we've got more than enough evidence," he muttered.

Wilkie cried all the way to Huston's place. At first, it was so soft that Pike barely heard him, then he would howl until Pike yelled, "Shut your mouth, you old fool. You asked for this." The drive was interminable. He couldn't stay far enough away from Wilkie to avoid his stench. The wind was in the wrong direction too, and that didn't help.

Tears coursed down Wilkie's cheeks, washing clean paths. "Help me," he begged. "You got to believe me. I told the truth. You can't blame an innocent man—"

Pike's repulsion was so great he was sickened with it. He would have liked to smash this old man's face. "You're a goddam liar," he said fiercely. "I saw you drive up right after Phil killed the steer. Nobody forced you to do anything. You had it all set up."

Wilkie looked at him with watery eyes. "What will he do to me?" he blubbered.

Pike had a bellyful of this sniveling wreck. "Even you ought to be smart enough to figure that out," he said with brutal candor.

Wilkie buried his face in his hands. The crying softened but never ceased.

Pike was grateful when the Huston soddy came into view. He wanted to get this morning over.

The Huston buggy was before the soddy, the old horse still in its shafts.

Cummings motioned Simmons to go around to the back to cover a rear door. Simmons came back a few seconds later and shook his head. This soddy had only one entrance.

"Jude," Cummings bawled. "Get out here. Right now."

Jude Huston came to the door, his face angry. Phil was right behind him.

Jude's anger faded as he saw who his visitor was and was replaced by uneasiness. His eyes flicked from rider to rider, and his unease grew. For a moment, he didn't see Wilkie's wagon behind the horsemen.

"What the hell," he complained. "Bellowing at a man like that."

"You two get out here," Cummings said harshly. "I won't tell you again."

Jude stepped outdoors, Phil a step behind him. "Pa, they got no call to be ordering us around like that," Phil said. His breathing was too fast, and his words jammed into each other.

Phil saw the wagon then, and his eyes went round in a face that turned deathly white. "Jesus, Pa," he bleated. "They've got Wilkie."

Jude was equally as pale. "Shut your damned mouth," he hissed. He stepped forward and looked up at Cummings. "Mr. Cummings, I don't know what he told you, but he's a liar."

"Shut up," Cummings roared. He puffed up with rage until he looked as though he would burst. He pulled his boot out of the stirrup, and for an instant, it looked as though he would kick Jude in the face.

Cummings slowly put the boot back. He had to control his breathing before he could talk. "You miserable bastard. You've been in with Wilkie from the start."

"Lies, lies," Jude said hoarsely. "I can prove it in any court. All I'm asking—" His voice faltered and died.

Cummings looked cruelly at him. "What makes you think you'll get as far as a court? Pike and Ord watched from the start. They saw Phil shoot the steer. You cut its throat. Then all three of you jumped in on the butchering."

Jude looked from face to face and saw no sympathy in any of them. He shut his eyes and swayed. It looked as though his legs were going to buckle and dump him. He opened his eyes and looked at his son. His eyes were sick, but he tried to grin.

"I guess they've got it all wrapped up, Phil. I guess this is the end of the road."

Phil clutched at his arm. "You've got to do something, Pa. You've got to—"

Jude had already made up his mind about the inevitability of the outcome, for he looked pityingly at Phil. "There ain't nobody who can do a damned thing. Nobody," he repeated with greater emphasis.

"Tie their hands," Cummings said frozenly.

Phil looked as though he wanted to try to make a break, and Cummings's words were a lash, peeling hide off Phil. "It wouldn't save you a thing. Go on, make a break for it. I'll shoot you in the leg. You'll still get what's coming to you."

Three pairs of hands were tied with strings cut off of saddles, then the Hustons and Wilkie were shoved toward the wagon. Phil fell twice before he reached the wagon. Each time, he was jerked back to his feet. His mouth hung slack and quivering, and he cried openly.

Wilkie was the last one to be helped into the bed of the wagon. Pike climbed onto the driver's seat and looked inquiringly at Cummings.

"Pike, we passed that big oak about a half mile back," Cummings said. "I think it's exactly what we're looking for."

Phil screamed then, high and shrill, sounding almost feminine.

"Get them out of here," Cummings said in disgust.

"You let my brother and father go," a high-pitched voice screamed. "You let them go."

All heads swiveled toward the soddy. Jonse stood in the doorway, trying to hold Phil's rifle steady against his shoulder. His withered arm made it difficult, and the muzzle waved in eccentric circles.

"I'll shoot you," Jonse shrilled.

The shadow of the doorway partially obscured him, making only one detail important. That was the rifle aimed at the five men.

Slaughter reacted without further thought. He clawed for his holster, drew, and fired a split-second after the gun was out. The impact of the bullet slammed Jonse back into the soddy. The rifle lay in the doorway where he dropped it.

Hannah screamed loud and piercingly, then called, "Jonse, Jonse." Her wailing never stopped.

Five heads turned and looked at each other. The savage moment laid its crushing weight on every face.

"You did it," Cummings shouted at Slaughter. "You shot that half-witted kid."

"Damn it," Slaughter said hotly. "All I saw was somebody standing in a doorway with a gun pointed at me. Did you think I was just going to sit here and do nothing?"

Nobody answered. Inman looked at the ground, his face wooden. Pike and Simmons looked at each other uncertainly.

This unexpected turn of events was having its effect on Cummings too, for he rolled his shoulders as though he was trying to shake something off of them.

"Maybe it'll save a lot of trouble in the long run," he said somberly. "He was a Huston. He'd grow up to be another thief, like the rest of them."

Hannah's crying went on and on. It had a keening sound, more animal-sounding than human.

Cummings listened to it a long moment, and it seemed to enrage him. "Are we going to sit around here all day? Let's get this over with."

Cummings had picked his tree well. A long, straight branch grew out from the trunk, and Cummings ordered the wagon stopped under the limb.

41

He untied his rope from the horn and demanded Pike's and Simmons's ropes. Simmons didn't want to give his up. "Hell, Brad, that's a brand new rope."

Cummings's grin was mirthless. "Then we don't have to worry about it breaking."

He didn't like the censure he saw in Simmons's eyes, for he said heatedly, "You'll get your damned rope back."

Simmons's face turned sullen. He started to say something, then decided against it and turned his face from Cummings.

Cummings fashioned three hangman's nooses and placed a loop over the heads of the Hustons and Wilkie. He tossed the remainder of the ropes over the branch and ordered Pike to tie the loose ends around the trunk.

Pike's stomach rolled uneasily as he went about his chore. He had seen a few hangings before, and even under the proper circumstances, it could make a man gag. All three of these thieves deserved hanging, but he had never really expected it to be handled this way. He thought Slaughter would have taken over and moved the prisoners into town for a legal hanging. Maybe the sheriff was too fearful to go up against what he saw in Cummings's face.

Pike kept swallowing to loosen up his throat. This was going to be a messy hanging. The wagon bed wasn't high enough from the ground to make the drop long enough to break a man's neck. When the drop was right, the neck was broken immediately, resulting in a quick and relatively merciful death. But if the neck wasn't broken, the victim dangled at the end of the rope and slowly strangled to death.

"Pike, will you move?" Cummings yelled.

Pike finished knotting the ropes and turned back toward the wagon.

"Lash that mule," Cummings ordered. "I want him to leave here in a hurry."

Slaughter held up his hand, checking Pike's move. "Do you any of you want to say anything?" he asked importantly.

Wilkie's eyes were closed. His lips moved as though he might be praying. If he heard Slaughter, he gave no indication.

Phil cried too hard to talk. Jude looked at Slaughter and inquired sullenly, "Would it do any good?"

"None," Slaughter replied.

"Then there ain't much sense in saying anything, is there?"

"Get on with it, Pike," Cummings yelled.

Pike lashed the mule with all the strength in his arm. It was probably the hardest the mule had been beaten in a long time. The mule squatted and twitched when Pike lashed him again. The mule sprang forward to get away from this merciless beating. Pike ran with him for a couple of steps, his arm rising and falling.

Pike stopped, breathing hard. The mule refused to go any faster. He didn't want to look behind him, but some awful fascination drew his eyes.

Three bodies dangled from the long branch. Except for a slight swaying at the end of the rope, Wilkie didn't move. He was the lightest and frailest of the three. He might have been lucky. The drop may have broken his neck.

The other two were kicking spasmodically, their legs drawing up, then kicking out convulsively. By their purpling faces Pike knew they were strangling.

He turned his head at a long, retching sound. Simmons's head was held low, and he was vomiting.

Pike felt his stomach roll and heave. If he looked at Jude and Phil any longer, he was going to be as violently sick as Simmons was.

"It had to be done," Cummings muttered.

Nobody made an answering comment.

# CHAPTER SIX

With his tongue lolling out, Dog loped along behind Gradie as he rode back toward Abilene. Eagle's pace wasn't too stiff for him. At least, he wasn't showing any distress.

Dog half irritated Gradie. It looked as though he didn't own the animal; Dog owned him. Gradie had seriously considered giving Dog to Jonse, but after Dog bit Phil, that was impossible. Phil would have killed the animal the first chance he had.

"Dog, you're a nuisance," Gradie muttered. Everything connected with his stop in Abilene was beginning to fall in that category. If he had been smart, he would have gone on back to Texas with Munn North. He said aloud with wry humor, "When did you ever consider yourself smart?"

His impulse to see his mother and Jonse had tied him up here; at least, for a while. He couldn't just ride off without giving them another thought, not after he saw the shape they were in. "Did you expect anything different?" he berated himself.

He rode into town and stopped at Arnold's store to buy some food to take out to the soddy. Rebellious thoughts troubled him, but there was no way he could rid himself of the knowledge that Jude and Phil would eat by far the greater percentage of that food. Gradie couldn't do anything about that. He grimaced at the thought. His resentment toward those two was still strong enough to begrude them a few mouthfuls of food.

Gradie dismounted and wrapped Eagle's reins around the hitching rack. He turned and waited for Dog to catch up with him. He roughed up Dog's head and said, "Don't try to come in with me." A storekeeper wouldn't appreciate Dog walking around and nosing everything in his store. He was damned sure that if any women customers were in the store, seeing Dog smelling over everything would horrify them. They would really be shocked, if Dog did what came naturally quite a few times a day to a male dog.

Dog followed him almost to the door. "No," Gradie said sternly. He put both hands on Dog's head and forced him into a sitting position. "Stay." He repeated the word several times, keeping pressure on Dog's head. When he removed his hands, Dog stayed put but whined deep in his throat.

Gradie looked back from the door. "Stay," he repeated and walked inside. There was no assurance Dog would stay there, but he was sort of proud at the obedience Dog was learning.

His long list of staples filled two gunny bags better than half full. Hannah probably needed everything she could get.

Arnold figured up his bill, and Gradie paid him. "Must be buying for a fair-sized family to order this much," he commented.

"Looks like it," Gradie agreed amiably. Arnold was fishing to find out what family Gradie was buying for.

Arnold's face showed disappointment as Gradie offered no information. "Sure feel like I should know you," he grumbled.

"Maybe you do," Gradie said lightly. He shouldered the two gunny bags and carried them out to the horse. Dog bounded up with joy at Gradie's appearance. His exuberance showed the depth of his worry that Gradie wouldn't come back. Dog had known enough loneliness.

Gradie tied the gunny bags together and slung them behind the saddle. Eagle's ears flicked back and forth. Gradie never knew what would displease him. Asking him to carry this new burden might be an insult to him.

"You buck these sacks off, and I'll kick hell out of you," Gradie said.

He hadn't missed the eager shine in Dog's eyes at the sight of the sacks. Gradie didn't know what he could smell in them. Maybe some instinct told the animal it was food. Dog had already eaten twice this day, but he was a fair-sized dog, and what he had eaten hadn't gone nearly far enough to fill up that belly, particularly when it had been empty for so long.

## The Grudge

Mrs. Caulkins's restaurant was across the street. Gradie walked toward it. He had never eaten here. The food might be bad, but that wouldn't matter to Dog.

"Stay," Gradie said outside the restaurant door. He pushed Dog down again.

Again Dog whined his worry, but he didn't move. Maybe his concern at Gradie's leaving had lessened a little.

It was between meals, and this was a slow time for a restaurant. Only one person was in the room, and she was busy, wiping off the table tops. She turned at Gradie's entrance, and looked unhappy at the intrusion.

"Supper's not for a couple of hours yet," she said crossly. "And I'm not cooking anything now."

She had an irascible temper, and Gradie wondered how much business she drove away. She was a plump woman with a heavy, unhappy face. Her hair was gray, and she moved as though her feet hurt. Maybe she was trying to make a living alone, Gradie thought. If so, she was going about it all wrong.

"Nothing for me, ma'am," he said. "But I'd like some scraps for my dog." At the irritation molding her face, he said quickly, "I intend to pay for whatever you have. Anything will do. Bones, stale bread." A ghost of a smile touched his lips as he remembered what he told Hannah about Dog. Dog would eat anything that wouldn't eat him.

"I'll see," Mrs. Caulkins said ungraciously. She came back from the kitchen, carrying a sack that was nearly filled. Under the other arm were three stale loaves of bread.

Gradie was pleased. He was sure for once, Dog would be filled.

She asked an outrageous fifty cents for scraps she would have thrown away. He paid the amount asked without comment.

Maybe she sensed the criticism in his manner, for she flushed. She followed him to the door, trying to justify her overcharge.

"I can't keep this business going by giving away everything," she said defensively.

"Sure," he replied woodenly.

Gradie stepped outside, and Dog went into his display of joy

47

again. Gradie broke one of the stale loaves and tossed Dog a chunk of it. A single gulp, and the chunk was gone.

"Is that what you bought those scraps for?" Mrs. Caulkins demanded indignantly.

Gradie looked at her, his eyebrows raising. She was heated over something.

"I won't have him around," she said shrilly. "I've run him off a hundred times. Always nosing around in my tin cans and garbage in the back. If you saw the mess he makes—" She had to take a deep breath before she could go on. "That ugly thing." Her voice kept rising. "Somebody ought to shoot him."

Dog nosed at Gradie's hand. He didn't want affection this time; he wanted food. Gradie tousled the big head. Dog was an ugly critter all right, but he had qualities that would put a lot of humans to shame.

Gradie stared levelly at Mrs. Caulkins. "Ma'am," he said in a soft voice, "we're lucky to have you around. You're purely filled with human kindness, aren't you?" He could have added to that, but he let it go.

"Come on, Dog," he said and moved on down the street. She got his meaning, for behind him, he heard her spluttering.

Dog bounded all around him. Something in that sack smelled fine, for he slavered and left wet spots on the walk. Gradie found an empty store after a block's walk, and sat down on the steps. He shouldn't be bothering anybody here. He fed the remains of the first loaf to Dog, and all it did was whet Dog's appetite for more. Gradie tore off chunks of the second loaf, reserving the bones and scraps for last. That should put Dog in canine heaven when Gradie dumped out the sack.

He let the meat scraps, bones, and the fat, fall on the bottom step and sat listening to Dog's eager slurping. Dog sure didn't have any manners.

Gradie's head raised as he heard a hesitant voice say, "Gradie?"

He had been so absorbed in watching Dog that he didn't hear the buckboard stop out in the street.

"Gradie," the voice repeated with the same hesitancy. "Is it you?"

Gradie stared gravely at the girl in the buckboard. His heart accelerated, picking up a heavy, pounding rhythm. He would have known her anyplace. This was the same Letty Cummings he remembered so well. Oh, changed some, but for the better.

He stood and advanced slowly to the buckboard. "Hello, Letty." She had matured and blossomed. He would be blind not to see the improvement.

"Gradie," she said and extended a hand. "It's so good to see you again." She ran her words together, and he thought there was a ragged catch in her breathing.

"You, too," he returned. Her eyes had an unnatural brightness, and there might be a sheen of moisture in them. He scoffed at that ridiculous impression. Seeing him wasn't going to make her cry.

"Are you gong to stay long?" She hadn't been able to conquer that breathlessness.

"For a while anyway," he said. "I saw Ma earlier. I've got to see her again."

"I'm glad you're back, Gradie." Her eyes touched his, then slid away.

She meant that, he thought in sudden jubilation. If ever there was a person filled with honesty, she was the one.

"Nobody knew you were coming," she said reproachfully.

"Didn't know myself until the last minute," he said cheerfully. "Your father knew I was here." He almost grinned at a fleeting thought. Brad Cummings would rather have a mouthful of manure than to say his name.

People across the street, had stopped to stare at them.

Gradie swore under his breath. It didn't take long to draw a crowd. A couple of people had stopped and stared, and their attention drew others. Now, eight or nine people stood over there, gawking at him and Letty. A few more seconds would double that number, for Gradie could see others coming this way. He couldn't see their lips move, but it didn't take much imagination to guess what those people were saying. Who was that talking to Letty Cummings? By God, Brad wouldn't like that when he heard about it. Letty Cummings had stopped right in the middle of the street to talk to a stranger. Someone or probably several in that small crowd would break their butts in getting the news to Cummings.

Gradie didn't want to cause Letty additional embarrassment. The longer he talked to her, the more the tongues would clack. He wanted to give her an opportunity to leave but didn't quite know how to do it without offending her.

"Letty, I've got to go. I hope I see you later." It was a lame, halting excuse, but he couldn't come up with anything better.

For a moment, she took his words at their face value, that he wanted to be rid of her, for her cheeks tightened. Then she realized he kept glancing across the street, and his face was growing cold and angry. Neither was directed at her. She turned her head and looked at the knot of people. A tinge of color rose in her throat as she realized she was the subject of their conjecture. The embarrassment had already started. She bit her lip, but her eyes blazed with defiance, and her chin had a proud lift.

"Is that a promise, Gradie?"

She had looked much the same the day Brad Cummings had kicked Gradie's ass down Texas Street. But there was one outstanding difference. She was no longer a helpless little girl.

"Yes." He drew a deep breath, and his eyes came alive. She was doing her best to tell him she wanted to see him again. "You can bet on it." There was no indecision in those words. He didn't know how or when he would see her, but he knew it would happen. He would do everything in his power to make it happen.

That faint, beautiful color was stealing into her face. "I'll hold you to it," she said. She gave him a flash of a radiant smile. She lifted the reins and drove on down the street.

Gradie stood where he was. His face froze again as he stared toward the curiosity seekers. He stared them down, and they moved restlessly. A small segment of them broke off and hurried up the street. Gradie didn't move until every one of them was gone.

The buckboard was out of sight when he turned to look down the street. "Did you gain a lot?" he asked himself. "You stared them down. Did it do you any good?" He didn't feel awkward or

50

childish. Yes, he had gained a lot. He wanted to yell with his newfound confidence. He had seen and talked to Letty, and she wanted it to happen again.

He turned back toward Dog. Dog was just finishing up the scraps, and he licked at the grease spot that was left on the step. For the first time, Gradie saw a different dimension he hadn't seen before in that belly. It was distended; that sunken appearance was gone.

Dog looked up at him, wagged his tail, then licked again at the grease spot.

"My God," Gradie said wonderingly. "Don't you ever get filled up?"

He walked back toward Eagle, confident Dog would follow him. Gradie grinned with a new humor. Dog was no dumb animal. He wasn't going to let go of the good thing he had found in Gradie.

Gradie swung into the saddle and turned Eagle back toward the soddy. Just that brief exchange with Letty had completely changed his outlook. On the way in to town, he had been resentful and bitter, begrudging the food Jude and Phil would eat. Now, he didn't give a damn. Nothing they could say or do was going to touch him again.

He shook Eagle into a canter. Dog was matching his pace to that of the horse. Gradie laughed aloud for no particular reason except that he just felt good.

"Dog," he called. "You're going to have to work off some of that belly now."

Gradie twisted and pulled at a problem as he rode. If he got a job around here, could he prevail on his mother and Jonse to leave Jude and Phil? It was certainly worth a try. With sour amusement, he thought, you might start out by asking Brad for a job.

He rode into the soddy's deserted yard. The old horse still stood in the shafts of the buggy, its head hanging low. Its weary look of resignation was probably acquired by spending too many hours like this.

Gradie's feeling of uneasiness returned. Something cold and slimy crawled up his arms. It was too quiet around here.

"Ma." He raised his voice. "Anybody home?"

# CHAPTER SEVEN

The sound of his own voice seemed to deepen and intensify the silence. "Ma," he called again. He started to swing down. He would look through the soddy, if he had to.

His boot touched the ground as Hannah appeared in the doorway. She walked unsteadily, and for a moment, he feared she was going to fall.

"Ma," he cried. "What's wrong."

Her hair was in complete disarray, and her face was ravaged by some kind of wild grief. She wasn't crying now, but her red-rimmed, swollen eyes showed that she had been. Her eyes shocked him the most. They were so crazed that he feared for her sanity.

Gradie sprang forward and took her in his arms. "Ma, what is it?"

He didn't think she understood him, and he shook her gently.

"Gradie," she moaned. Her fingers bit into his arm with surprising strength. "Jonse's dead."

What he feared had happened. Her sanity was gone. She couldn't mean what she was saying.

"You're wrong, Ma," he said. "I saw him a short while ago."

"He's dead, Gradie." Her voice and face were lifeless. "He's inside. You can see for yourself."

Her eyes closed tightly, and she swayed. Gradie thought she was going to fall, but she reached out and found a new strength from some source he couldn't see.

"Go see," she whispered. "I'll wait here." Tears welled up into her eyes but didn't brim over. The well had run almost dry.

Gradie left his mother standing beside the buggy and walked toward the soddy. Just inside the door he stopped to adjust his

53

eyes to the shadowy interior. Jonse lay a dozen feet from the doorway. The earthen floor was scuffed up, as though he had dragged his feet before he fell. A rifle lay between him and the doorway. Oh God, Gradie thought in horror. He was fooling with that rifle and shot himself. Jonse lay on his back, his sightless eyes focused on the ceiling.

Gradie stared down at him, his mind frozen in an icy grip. The only pitiful consolation in this tragic matter was that Jonse hadn't known pain long. The wound was in his chest, and from the location, Gradie would say Jonse had died instantly.

How could Jonse have shot himself with that rifle? With his withered arm, it seemed almost impossible that Jonse could have handled and fired the rifle with one good hand.

He squatted down and frowned at the wound. That didn't look like a rifle wound to him. He straightened, his mind reeling. He had no idea of how long Hannah had been by herself with Jonse. His face twisted savagely. Where in the hell were Jude and Phil.

He stripped a blanket off of one of the beds and covered Jonse, then picked up the rifle. The muzzle smelled of burnt gunpowder. This gun had been fired, how recently he couldn't tell. He didn't know how, but Jonse had managed to kill himself with it.

He walked outside, and Hannah watched him approach. "Where were Jude and Phil?" he demanded as he reached her. "Why did they let him play with that rifle?"

She shuddered, and her face twisted. She looked as though she had aged twenty years.

"Jonse didn't shoot himself," she whispered.

Gradie had to bend his head close to catch what she said. Her voice was fragile, sounding as though it would shatter into myriad pieces.

He gripped her shoulders tightly. "Easy, Ma." She sounded as though something inside might let go at any split second, sending her into hysteria.

She looked up into his face and shook her head. "I know what you're thinking, Gradie. But I'm better now. I sat there so long with Jonse." A wonder was evident in her voice. "If I got through that, I'll be all right."

"Ma," he begged. "Will you tell me what happened?"

She nodded dully. "I saw it all." Her voice sounded like the faint, dry rasp of dead leaves, rubbing together. "They came after Jude and Phil."

His mind was staggered by facts he couldn't connect. Jonse was dead, and somebody came after Jude and Phil. "Who are you talking about? Why did they come here?"

She twisted her hands. "I begged Jude to stop. I knew he'd be caught. But he wouldn't listen."

Gradie gripped her shoulders. "Ma," he said imploringly.

"It was Sheriff Slaughter and his deputy, Inman. Cummings brought two of his riders with him. I only knew the one called Pike."

Gradie had more facts, but nothing seemed to fit. "Why were they here?"

"They came after Jude and Phil," she whispered.

"Why?" he asked frantically.

"For rustling. They killed one of Brad Cummings's cattle. It wasn't the first time."

Gradie's mouth sagged. "Oh, my God," he exploded. "The damned fools."

She nodded numb agreement. "I begged them to stop. They've been doing it for over a year. They wouldn't listen to me. Jude said it was our living. He said we had a right—"

Her voice trailed away.

"Go on," he said savagely.

"The sheriff had Old man Wilkie and his wagon. The butchered animal was in the wagon." A shudder ran through her, and her eyes were huge in a gaunt face. "They took them away to hang them, Gradie. I saw them tie their hands."

Gradie made an impatient gesture. He could feel no sorrow for Jude and Phil. They had earned this. They were lucky to have gotten away with rustling as long as they had.

"Where does Jonse fit in this?"

A tiny wail escaped her, and he thought the tears would come again. "Jonse grabbed up Phil's rifle. He ran to the door and screamed they weren't going to take his father and brother."

Anguish twisted her face, and she wrung her hands. "I was too far away to stop Jonse, Gradie. Sheriff Slaughter whipped his head around, saw Jonse, and drew his gun. He killed Jonse." The tears came again and ran down her cheeks. "Jonse couldn't have used that rifle. He couldn't, not with his bad arm."

Gradie wanted to drive his fist into something. He wanted to rave and swear, and he stifled the impulse. He forced himself into thinking rationally. He could understand how it happened. All Slaughter had seen was a gun threatening him, and he had reacted. He had shot Jonse without checking further. Legally, Slaughter was blameless. Gradie's eyes smoldered. The morality of the incident was another matter.

Hannah buried her face against his chest, and Gradie let her cry. He patted her shoulder. His mind was empty. He couldn't think of a thing to say that would bring her any comfort.

She finally raised her tear-ravaged face, and he handed her a bandanna. "I want you to take the buggy and go into town, Ma."

The protest formed in her face, and he said firmly, "You're going. If you're thinking of Jonse, I'll take care of him. Go to the Drovers' Cottage. I'll find you there."

She wanted to go back into the soddy, and he talked her out of that. "Ma, I can come back later and get anything you need." He pressed some money into her hand. "For the hotel," he said, stopping her words.

He waited until she was in the buggy before he asked, "Which way did they take Pa and Phil?"

A tremor ran through her, but her voice was steady enough. "That way, Gradie," she said, pointing. "I don't know exactly where."

Gradie nodded. Wagon tracks led off in the direction Hannah indicated.

Gradie waited until Hannah turned the buggy and headed for town before he started out. The wagon tracks weren't difficult to follow. Hoofprints were on either side of the wagon tracks. What terror Jude and Phil must have known while taking this trip. "The poor damned fools," he muttered. It was as close to pity as he could come.

56

He saw the tree from quite a way off. If he hadn't known what those grisly, dangling objects were, he would not have been able to identify them as bodies without getting closer.

He glanced only briefly at the three hanged men before he looked away. Jude and Phil had died hard. He didn't know the third one. That had to be the old man Hannah spoke of.

Gradie couldn't feel the slightest pull of grief. The bond that was the basis for such grief had been severed quite a few years back, even before Gradie left Abilene. He was a cattleman himself, and he could understand what motivated Cummings. But Cummings had to be a dirty bastard to go away and leave three men like this. The four-legged and the winged predators would tear the bodies apart before the night was out.

Gradie resolutely kept from looking up into the sky. He wouldn't have been surprised to see buzzards already circling.

Gradie's work was cut out for him, but he didn't quite know how to go about it. Jude and Phil were heavy men and would be hard to handle. Wilkie was on the small side. But what would Gradie do with them after he cut the three down? Even if he could get Jude or Phil onto Eagle's back, it was doubtful that the gelding would permit the body to stay there long. The horse had an aversion to carrying burdens other than saddle and rider. Even if the horse permitted placing a body on his back, it would take a wearying time to get all three bodies into town, making three separate trips. Gradie thought of Jonse and amended his thinking. He would have to make four trips.

He looked around, not in the particular hope of seeing help, but with a sort of futility that was only delaying coming to immediate grips with his problem. His face brightened. There was a wagon, some quarter of a mile to the southwest. An animal still stood in the shafts. Hannah had spoken of a wagon. This had to be the one.

Gradie rode up to the wagon and evaluated the old, tired mule. No wonder the mule hadn't run farther.

He looked at the cargo the wagon carried and shook his head at the sight of the butchered meat. "The poor damned fools," he said again, but there was no real sympathy in the words.

Hordes of flies buzzed angrily as Gradie climbed into the wagon bed. He threw and kicked the meat out onto the ground.

Dog hesitated before he jumped on the meat. "It's all yours, Dog," Gradie muttered. Dog could gorge himself until he wouldn't be able to drag. Gradie would rather see Dog get some of the meat instead of leaving it all for the predators.

He tied Eagle to the back of the wagon, climbed onto the seat, and drove the mule back toward the tree. He looked back. Dog watched him, suffering an agony of indecision. Dog would lift his head, stare at Gradie, then lower it to tear off another mouthful of meat. Gradie nearly smiled. Dog didn't know whether to stay with the meat, or go with him.

Gradie drove a little beyond the three bodies, then backed the wagon up, looking constantly behind him to be sure he was positioning the wagon accurately. The end of the bed hit Phil's boots first, for they dangled below the height of the bed. Gradie halted the mule, walked back, and lifted and pushed Phil's legs as far as he could into the wagon. It saved him from having to lift all of Phil's weight.

He had to repeat that procedure three times before he got all three bodies positioned over the wagon bed.

When he reached the trunk of the tree, he pulled a knife from his pocket. Damned thing was getting rusty, and Gradie swore at its stubbornness. He broke a thumb nail getting a blade open.

A cold rage filled him by the time the knife was opened; at himself, at Cummings, at Slaughter, at his father and brother. His rage included everything and everybody involved in this miserable business.

The ropes were new and stout, and it took vigorous sawing with the knife to cut the first rope. Gradie cursed himself for carrying a dull knife.

A brief glance at the wagon and the dull thud as the rope parted, assured him that Phil's body had fallen onto the wagon bed.

The other two ropes were as difficult to cut as the first one. This time, Gradie didn't look around as the two bodies dropped into the wagon.

He removed the three ropes from the bodies and flung them on the ground. His rage mounted until he was shaking uncontrollably. The anguish stamped on each face and the vicious, burned weal on each neck sickened him.

He climbed back to the wagon seat and turned the mule toward the soddy. There was one other thing to do before he could get out of this hellish period of time that never seemed to end.

He stopped before the soddy. Dog whined and licked his hand. Gradie hadn't thought to check and see if Dog was following him. But Dog had made his own decision.

Gradie walked into the soddy, tucked the blanket tighter around Jonse, then carried him out to the wagon. He placed him as far away as he could from the other three.

The desire to strike out and drive his fists into something was almost overwhelming. If only he could scream at the senseless pattern of the world. Jonse had no part, no blame in this, but the price demanded included him.

Gradie lifted the reins, but before he snapped them against the mule's rump, he glanced down at Dog. Dog looked up at him, his eyes trying to say something.

"Do you want to ride, Dog?"

Dog whined his eagerness.

"Well, come on then," Gradie said roughly.

Dog bounded upward, almost making the seat with one leap. Gradie heard the scrape of the dog's toenails. He reached out, grabbed him by the scruff of the neck, and dragged into a more secure position.

Dog tried to lick his face. Gradie pushed him away. "No, not now." He started the wagon and placed an arm about Dog's neck. Dog squirmed with delight.

"This is an easier trip for you, than for the others," Gradie said. He thought of Hannah, of Jonse, and of himself, then of the four behind him. Dog was the only one who was having an easy trip.

# CHAPTER EIGHT

Gradie wondered if Compton's undertaking parlor was still in town. He turned off of Texas Street. Yes, the faded sign over a building a half block down said that Compton was still here. The sign advertised inexpensive, efficient and sympathetic service. Gradie had been here only once before, but he still remembered it well. He had been six years old when his cousin died from a rattlesnake bite. That bad time had never left his mind. Compton had handled that funeral. Gradie hoped he would handle this one, too.

He walked into the dreary little office, and Travis Compton looked up from his desk, an inquring look on his face. The questioning look changed to a puzzled frown.

Gradie knew the cause of that frown. Compton was trying to recognize him.

"Do I know you?" Compton asked.

"Maybe," Gradie said shortly. Compton would learn who he was quick enough. "I want to arrange for three funerals."

Compton blinked. This was a rush of business. He donned his sympathetic, professional manner. "Ah, I am sorry, Mr.—" He waited, but Gradie didn't fill in a name. Compton sighed and went on, "Where do you want the deceased picked up?"

"From the wagon just outside," Gradie responded. "You'll need somebody to help me carry them in. Unless you can do it." Compton didn't look very capable. Compton had picked up a tremendous amount of weight since Gradie had seen him, and he looked as soft as a bowl of mush.

Compton made a deprecatory move with his hand. "No problem. Henry's in the back room." He raised his voice. "Henry! A gentleman needs help."

Henry came into the room. He was powerfully muscled, but his eyes were dull in a blank face. Gradie suspected that digging graves had built up those shoulders and arms.

Gradie led the way out to the wagon, Compton and Henry on his heels.

Compton looked into the wagon and gulped. "These men have been hanged," he said in a horror-filled voice.

"They have," Gradie said tonelessly. Compton hadn't missed those purplish weals on the three dead men's necks.

Compton looked helplessly at Gradie. He coughed, clearing his throat, and said, "Jude and Phil Huston. The third one is Old man Wilkie."

"You called them right," Gradie said harshly. "If you want to know more about them, ask Slaughter. He can tell you all about it. Jonse Huston is under the blanket. I'll carry him in. Wilkie stays out here. I've got another place for him."

Compton looked distressed. Gradie wondered cynically, if it hurt Compton to lose any part of this business.

Gradie gently lifted Jonse out of the wagon and carried him inside. Compton directed him to a table in the rear room. Gradie put Jonse on the table and folded the blanket back. Jonse's face wasn't peaceful. He had known savage, jolting pain before he died. Gradie again knew the desire to rave and swear at the unfairness of the world. Jonse hadn't had much of a life or a long one.

Henry came in carrying Jude. It didn't seem as though it cost him much effort. Henry was a horse for work.

Compton cleared his throat. He wanted to say something, but he was finding it difficult.

"Is this what's bothering you?" Gradie asked. He pulled money from his pocket and waited for Compton to name a figure.

Compton hesitated, and Gradie thought, he's trying to name a figure that I won't squawk about too much. A figure almost slipped out of Compton's mouth, then he looked at those cold, emotionless eyes and hastily changed his mind. He called off an amount and weakly asked, "Is that all right with you?"

Gradie nodded and counted out bills into Compton's hand. "I want the funeral in the morning."

Compton bleated as though he had been stabbed. "Tomorrow morning? I can't possibly make—"

"Afternoon then." Gradie cut him short. He started toward the door, then stopped. Henry came back, carrying Phil.

Gradie waited until Henry disappeared into the rear room. He stared at Compton then said, "You've been wondering who I am. I'm Gradie Huston."

Compton's mouth slowly opened until it formed an O.

"I want everything done right," Gradie said.

"I can promise you—"

Gradie turned before Compton could get all of the sentence out. As he went through the door, Compton was still talking.

Gradie drove the wagon to Slaughter's office. Three men were in the room, all wearing badges. Two of the badges said DEPUTY. Gradie hadn't seen any of these men before.

Gradie looked at Slaughter. Slaughter didn't know him either, but his eyes were wary.

"I'm bringing back something that belongs to you," Gradie snapped. Gradie didn't miss the exchange of looks between the three. Slaughter was a short, blocky man. The shadow of encroaching fat was already thickening his neck. The tall deputy had a tough face and arrogance that stuck out all over him. The third deputy was somewhere around Gradie's age.

"What belongs to me?" Slaughter rasped. His hands rested on the desk, but there wasn't anything relaxed about them.

"A dead man and a wagon and mule," Gradie snapped.

Slaughter's eyes widened. "Just a damned minute—"

Gradie's tone was a whip, lashing through Slaughter's words. "You've had a busy day, haven't you, Sheriff? You hanged three men and shot a crippled kid. That ought to keep you polishing your badge for a long time."

Slaughter stared at him, then flushed. He tried to meet Gradie's eyes and failed. "I don't know what you mean," he mumbled.

"You lying to me, or yourself?" Gradie challenged.

The tall deputy resented Gradie's words. He bent forward

menacingly and roared, "Who the hell do you think you are, coming in here and talking like that?"

"That's enough, Inman," Slaughter barked.

"Slaughter knows what I'm talking about," Gradie said. "And he knows who I am."

"Old man Wilkie's in the wagon," Gradie said. He liked the harried flash in Slaughter's eyes. "Getting him buried is your problem. I don't give a damn who pays for it."

Slaughter flashed Gradie a hasty glance then looked at his desk. If he had any argument against what Gradie was saying, he choked it back.

Inman's perception wasn't as quick as Slaughter's. He had to have things spelled out for him. "Who's taking care of the other two?"

The rake of Gradie's eyes was an open affront.

Inman flushed and said heatedly, "Goddammit. I asked—"

"You've got a fat mouth, Deputy," Gradie said with slow deliberation that added to his former insult. "Also a slow mind to go with it. I'm taking care of them."

Inman's face flushed instantly. "Why, goddam you. Nobody talks to me like—"

Slaughter half raised himself out of his chair. He raked Inman with a savage look. "I told you to stay out of this," he yelled.

A murderous flare appeared briefly in Inman's eyes, then he stared sullenly at the floor.

Gradie saw that was going to hold Inman. He spun on his heel and walked toward the door.

"He's one of the Hustons," Slaughter said in a low tone, but his words carried to Gradie. "Cummings told me this morning he was back. You leave him alone until I find out what Brad wants to do about him."

Gradie's lips curled as he walked out of the office. His identification was all straightened out now. He hadn't the slightest idea of what would happen from here on.

The Hustons' funeral was poorly attended. Gradie had found a preacher to say a few words over the three coffins. Compton was there, attending to his business. Henry was there to assist him. Hannah and Gradie stood at Jonse's graveside. Jonse's death was the one that really crushed Hannah. Gradie's heart ached for her. Her face was drawn and pale, though she didn't cry. Gradie thought the final tear was drained out of her.

He listened absently to the preacher's fumbling attempt to find something laudatory to say about the Hustons. The preacher was making heavy weather of it. Gradie guessed the most difficult part would be trying to manufacture good things to say when they didn't exist. The preacher finally cut the halting words short. Gradie was grateful it was over.

He took Hannah's arm to turn and lead her away. He didn't want her staying here while the graves were being filled.

Dog joined them, whining as he thrust his nose against Hannah's hand. She stroked him absently. "He's so ugly, isn't he?" she said calmly. "But Jonse thought he was beautiful."

"Yes," Gradie said. Whatever else he wanted to say was wiped away by the appearance of Slaughter's third deputy. The deputy had stayed in the background, but Gradie supposed he had been here all during the service. His face blackened. Slaughter wasn't content with what he had already done, now he was having his deputy watch Gradie.

The outrage rose in successive waves, until Gradie thought he would choke.

Hannah walked with her eyes downcast. She hadn't as yet seen the deputy. Gradie had to struggle to subdue his wrath. Hannah had enough grief without the deputy adding more unpleasant moments to her burden.

The deputy stepped forward to intercept them. He must have noticed Gradie's set expression, but it didn't deter him.

Dog came up to the deputy and sniffed around his legs. Gradie half hoped Dog would take a chunk out of him. Dog's hackles didn't even rise. He kept up his sniffing, and his tail wagged. Gradie felt like booting the animal. Dog's instincts were poor.

"Mrs. Huston," the deputy said softly. "I'm powerfully sorry. If there's anything I can do—". He couldn't find a way to finish the sentence, and he let the words die.

Gradie searched the words and tone. He couldn't find a thing wrong with either of them. The deputy meant what he said.

Hannah's head lifted. "Thank you, Cal. Gradie, this is Cal Daugherty. He's been a good friend to us. For a while, his family lived nearby."

Gradie accepted the proffered hand. There was no malice in those eyes. He looked at a frank, open face with no deceit or arrogance in it. Evidently, he hadn't worked long enough for Slaughter for the sheriff's bad traits to have rubbed off on him.

"Your mother's got that wrong," Daugherty said gruffly. "She's been the real friend to us. She nursed Ma when she was so bad sick a couple of years ago. If it hadn't been for her, Ma wouldn't have pulled through."

Gradie felt a loosening go through him. He had judged on surface impressions, and he was all wrong. The last of Gradie's resentment toward Daugherty because he wore a badge, vanished.

"Thank you," Gradie said almost without stiffness.

"I'm sorry for all your trouble," Daugherty said sincerely. His vague gesture was meant to include many things. He stopped, at a loss for words. "Let me know, if there's anything I can do for you," he said lamely.

"Sure," Gradie said. Dog's instincts weren't bad after all.

The word gave Daugherty his release. He ducked his head in sudden embarrassment, whirled, and strode rapidly away.

"Cal wasn't with Slaughter and Inman yesterday," Hannah said. "Maybe he knew what they intended to do and refused to go with them."

Gradie nodded. If that was the explanation for Daugherty's absence, he wouldn't last long with Slaughter.

Gradie didn't want to think any more about Abilene's law, or Brad Cummings. He couldn't point an accuisng finger at Slaughter, or Cummings for that matter. The sooner he closed the door on the whole thing and dismissed it from his mind the better off he would be. He hoped Hannah could do the same thing, though he couldn't tell about her. Her thoughts were locked up behind that blank face.

"Ma," he asked, "what do you want to do now?"

Gradie meant in the future, but Hannah took his question to mean now. "Gradie, I'd just like to lay down for a while. I'm so tired I can't think."

"Whatever you want, Ma," he said in instant understanding. She needed time before she could even begin to think of what she was going to do. Gradie would give her two or three days before he brought up the subject again. When her thoughts were in order, he hoped that she would want to leave Abilene. There certainly wasn't anything here to hold either of them.

"We'll go back to the Drovers' Cottage, Ma. You lay down and sleep as much as you want. I'll be by for you at suppertime."

Gradie left her at the hotel and walked down the street. Another chore was ahead of him, one that he dreaded almost as much as the funerals. He would have to take Hannah out to the soddy to get the things she wanted to save. That would bring the whole sorry matter vividly to life again, reopening the old wounds. There was no way to avoid that trip. What he needed most at the moment was a stiff drink.

# CHAPTER NINE

Gradie was aware of the covert glances of the people he passed. Maybe it's Dog that's pulling attention, he thought. But he knew that wasn't it. By now, everybody in Abilene had heard what had happened to the Huston place. He could just imagine people saying, "That's him; the last of the Hustons. He's lucky he wasn't out there when it happened, or he'd have been hanged too."

Gradie forced his clenched hands open. Give a dog a bad name— The unfinished thought brought a wry grin to his lips. He watched Dog bound ahead of him, then turn and race back. A lot of people in Abilene didn't like Dog, but the animal simply didn't care, or was unaware of the hostility. Gradie wished he could feel the same way. Actually, he didn't give a damn what any of these people thought. They could point their fingers at him all they wanted to, but they weren't going to do it to his face. He was through taking any accusing or contemptuous talk from anybody. An individual didn't have to have a hand in what happened to turn a town against him; just the wrong name was enough. The town joined solidly against an underdog, and nobody checked to see if the accusation was fair or unjust.

"Like a bunch of wild dogs," Gradie muttered. "They don't have to see what or why they're chasing something. All they need is a scent—"

Dog came racing back and licked Gradie's hand.

"Dog, I apologize to you for that," Gradie said.

He grinned twistedly. He was wrong in saying everybody in Abilene had turned solidly against him because he was named Huston. Cal Daugherty didn't feel that way. But one person's feeling didn't make much of a dent against the hostility of an entire town.

A buckboard passed him, going the opposite way. Gradie kept his face blank, though it was hard to keep his pleasure from showing at seeing Letty again. But he knew better than to wave or call to her. Brad Cummings drove the buckboard. Gradie didn't want the slightest thing to cause Letty embarrassment or trouble.

Gradie heard the buckboard stop. He didn't even look around when he heard the vehicle back up. He knew Letty had no hand in that action. Cummings wouldn't have stopped for her, even if she begged him. No, the backing had to be Cummings's doing. This could spell trouble. Gradie didn't want to see or talk to Brad Cummings.

"Dog." He raised his voice, calling Dog back to him. He walked with his hand on Dog's head. He was pretty certain what Dog's reaction would be, if Cummings tried to get tough with Gradie. Dog had taken a piece out of Phil. The memory gave Gradie a sour pleasure. But he would try to restrain Dog from doing the same with Cummings, just because Letty was along.

Gradie kept on walking, even when the buckboard was opposite him.

"Huston," Cummings roared. "I want to talk to you."

Dog snarled softly in his throat. Gradie pressed his hand harder on Dog's head. He didn't respond to Cummings by speaking or slowing his step.

Cummings called him a name. Gradie's cheeks tightened. He didn't respond to the name, either, though his breathing quickened. Cummings was bent on trouble. Because Letty was along, Gradie would ignore everything he possibly could just to save her distress.

Cummings's boots thudded against the street as he jumped from the buckboard, then Gradie heard the rapid footsteps behind him. Dog wanted to whip about. Gradie's hold on that shaggy lock of hair prevented Dog from breaking loose.

"Papa," Letty called. She sounded frantic.

Gradie didn't hear Cummings respond to that plea. He doubted if Cummings even bothered to look at her. He heard a faster rush of boots on the walk.

"Goddam you," Cummings yelled. "When I tell you something, you listen."

A hand grabbed Gradie by an elbow.

Gradie whirled, twisting the hand loose, and lost his hold on Dog. Dog was crouched close to the walk, every fang in his head showing.

"No," Gradie said sharply to Dog before he turned to face Cummings again. "You came damned close to losing that hand. He was ready to bite it off."

Cummings saw the menace in the crouched, snarling dog, for some of the color left his face. "Why, I'll blow his goddam head off."

"You try, and you're a dead man," Gradie said levelly. He was losing his grip on his mounting temper. He was rapidly getting beyond the point of caring where this went from here on. It was too bad that Letty was here to see what developed, but he couldn't help that.

Cummings's breath came faster, and he was so damned mad he sprayed out flecks of spit when he tried to talk.

"Are you trying to threaten me?" he asked jerkily.

Gradie's voice didn't change. "Take it any way you want."

Already, this confrontation was drawing attention. Gradie heard voices raised up and down the block, then the sound of running feet. There was no doubt where the townspeople's allegiance lay. It wouldn't be long before he had a ring of hostile eyes around him.

Gradie waited for Cummings's next move, and he didn't much care what it was. Cummings was armed. Gradie sincerely wished that Cummings's rage wouldn't drive him into something as foolish as reaching for his gun. But Gradie could see words weren't going to satisfy Cummings's anger. If he didn't try to use his gun, he would try to use his fists, or his boots. An old memory twisted violently in Gradie. Cummings had used his boots once before. Surely, Cummings wouldn't be that big a damned fool to try that again.

Cummings spluttered, trying to find the words to express his fury.

Gradie had a hold of that shaggy lock of hair again. "Quiet," he said again. Dog ignored the order. He wouldn't stop his snarling.

"Why don't you get out of here before you're in real trouble?" Gradie said coldly. "I don't know how much longer I can hold him."

Gradie heard the lighter rush of feet. He wasn't facing the buckboard, but he knew that had to be Letty. Stay out of this, Letty, he groaned.

Cummings's eyes were hot coals, and he had trouble with his breathing. "By God, if you think you can talk to me like—"

Letty passed her father, breaking off his words. She stepped in between him and Gradie. She glanced at Gradie and the dog, then put all of her attention on her father. "Stop this," she said indignantly.

That startled Gradie. He didn't think she had enough backbone to stand up to Cummings like this.

Cummings's mouth sagged. Evidently, he was surprised too. "Just a minute," he blurted.

"I mean it, Papa," she said firmly. "I saw it all. You started it. If that dog bites you, it'll be solely your fault." Her anger was as great as her father's, but she expressed it differently. A sheen of tears was in her eyes, and her cheeks were rigid and pale. "You stopped Gradie. You started all this." She looked around. People were close to them now. Some of them were already crossing the street. She lowered her voice. "If you don't leave now, I'll tell everybody exactly how this got started." Her chin had a belligerent jut. "Do you want me to do that?"

He looked from his daughter to Gradie, then at Letty again. "We'll talk about this later," he said grimly. He turned his head toward Gradie. Gradie had never seen a meaner, colder pair of eyes. "You ain't heard the last of this, either."

Hot words trembled on Gradie's tongue, but Letty's eyes pleaded with him. His nod was barely perceptible. He owed her something. He spun on his heel and continued on his way, brushing aside two men who had just arrived. He didn't turn his head as Cummings swore at the buckboard horse and lashed it with the whip. The sharp clatter of hoofs told how stinging that whiplash had been.

Gradie still wanted that drink, but he better change his plans. Dog's reaction toward Cummings told him that. Dog was ready to take anybody who showed any animosity toward Gradie. Gradie thought he had better leave Dog in a safer place, particularly while he was in the saloon.

He changed his course, turning toward the livery stable. Dog could stay with Eagle; the two got along well enough.

"Can I leave him here?" Gradie asked Sawyer.

Sawyer looked at Dog with a jaundiced eye. "I don't want him roaming around here," he said sourly.

"He won't be," Gradie snapped. "I'll leave him in Eagle's stall."

After some consideration, Gradie received reluctant consent. Sawyer found a piece of rope. Gradie tied one end of it around Dog's neck, then secured him in the stall. Dog's whining didn't stop Gradie from leaving.

"You old cuss," he said. "I'll be back pretty soon." He wished he could explain to Dog, that if he was going to walk around town with him, he couldn't jump on everybody who didn't like Gradie.

Gradie thought about Cummings as he continued on his way toward the Bull Head. That pigheaded old fool didn't realize how much he owed his daughter. She had stopped a brawl between them and no doubt her action had saved her father actual hurt. Gradie knew he wouldn't have taken any verbal or physical abuse from Cummings.

Gradie walked into the Bull Head and took a place at the far end of the bar. Business was slow, and the bartender broke off his conversation with the only two customers in the place and moved toward Gradie. His annoyance at having to move this far showed.

The bartender was a short, beefy man with a red face. For a moment, Gradie thought the man's belligerence was because he knew who Gradie was. He locked eyes with the bartender, and the man's surliness eased off.

"Whiskey," Gradie ordered. He made no attempt to keep the bite out of his voice.

His tone changed the bartender's mind. "Yes, sir," he said and turned to get a bottle from the back bar. Gradie watched his reflection in the back mirror. The bartender had a puzzled look on his face every time he stole a glance at Gradie.

Gradie made the first drink last a good while, then ordered another one. He felt lonely and depressed. He was caught in a hole that seemed to grow deeper. He wished he and Hannah were leaving Abilene tonight, but he couldn't suggest that to her; not for a few more days. She was emotionally and physically drained; she needed time to recover from the spiritual battering she had taken. She won't find that needed peace here, Gradie thought angrily. But he knew he wouldn't be able to pry her away from Jonse's grave; not for a little while anyway.

Cal Daugherty came into the saloon. He saw Gradie, and his intention to join him was plain on his face. Gradie shook his head, the gesture stopping Daugherty. He appreciated what Daugherty was trying to do, but it wouldn't do Daugherty any good to get in bad with the rest of the town because of Gradie.

Gradie's dismissal put a small frown on Daugherty's face. Gradie noticed the stiffness in his cheeks. Daugherty didn't understand, or like what Gradie did. He took a place halfway down the bar and ordered a beer.

The bartender drew the beer and said, "A big funeral this afternoon, Cal."

Daugherty emptied half of his glass before he spoke. "I wouldn't know what you mean, Gill."

"Sure, you do," Gill argued. "Burying all them Hustons. Brad did the country a good service by getting rid of them."

Color crept slowly up Daugherty's neck. He finished the beer and shoved the glass at Gill. "Another beer," he said savagely.

Gill gave him an astonished glance, refilled the glass, and shoved it back toward Daugherty. The more he thought about Daugherty's reaction, the more upset he became. It showed on his face.

"Hell, Cal," he said argumentatively. "You sound like you're sorry about the Hustons."

Daugherty fixed him with a long, level stare. "I just don't see any damned sense rehashing it over and over. It's over with and done."

Gill had a belligerent disposition, for his jaw jutted. "Are you trying to tell me I can't talk about it any more?"

The muscles along Daugherty's jaw bunched and jerked. "I'm telling you for your own good," he said quietly. "If you had an ounce of brains, you'd let it drop."

Gill spluttered and spumed. "You can't stop me from talking about what I please."

"Maybe not," Daugherty agreed almost pleasantly. "But there's somebody in here who can." He gave the statement a significant pause, then added, "That's Gradie Huston at the end of the bar."

Gill's head whipped toward Gradie. His face seemed to lose all the bone behind it, for it turned loose and flabby. He ducked his head to avoid meeting Gradie's eyes. "Hell," he mumbled. "I didn't mean no particular harm."

Gradie finished his drink. He wanted to throw the glass through the back mirror. Instead, he carefully set it down. It wouldn't do him any good to start a row in here.

He nodded to Daugherty and started away from the bar. His decision to leave came too late. Brad Cummings was just coming in through the swinging doors.

# CHAPTER TEN

Gradie turned back and leaned against the bar, hoping that Cummings wouldn't notice him. If Cummings got interested in drinking, maybe Gradie could slip out unnoticed.

He watched Cummings in the back mirror. Cummings tossed down two quick shots. He must want to keep a fire under the head of steam he already had. Gill showed great deference in serving him, and the two original customers made every effort to be agreeable.

Gradie knew a small regret. It was very unlikely he could slip out before Cummings became aware of his presence. In fact, he was surprised that Cummings's head hadn't turned toward him by now.

Daugherty's reaction toward Cummings surprised Gradie. He hadn't moved to join the people fawning over Cummings; he hadn't even tried to speak to him. Apparently, Daugherty didn't have much liking for Brad Cummings. Gradie thought with wry humor, at least, we think alike on that score.

In the mirror, he saw Gill bend far over the bar and say something in Cummings's ear. The furtiveness of his manner warned Gradie. It's coming now, he thought resignedly. He knows I'm here. For Letty's sake he regretted what could happen. He had run once before from Cummings; it would not happen again.

He heard the heavy thud of boots as they came toward him. They stopped, but Gradie didn't look around. It was too bad a man didn't have the power to wish another one far away.

"You'll talk to me now," Cummings said with mean satisfaction.

Gradie swung around from the bar. He put his elbows on it and

77

leaned back. "We haven't got a damned thing to talk about," he said flatly.

There was no doubt about Cummings being drunk now. His eyes were red-rimmed, and he swayed a little. Letty's interference had only made him that much more furious. Maybe the two drinks he had here weren't all he'd had; maybe he'd stopped in another place. It didn't matter. The whiskey in him was making him boiling mad.

"Don't tell me what we've got to talk about," Cummings yelled. "I've had a bellyful of you Hustons for too long. Damned thieves. You've robbed me blind."

Gradie didn't point out the exaggeration of those words, though he couldn't question the justice of that accusation. Over Cummings's shoulder, Gradie saw the customers and Gill staring at them. Daugherty had moved until he stood just a step behind Cummings.

Gradie's hold on his temper was spiderweb fragile, but he tried to talk some reason into Cummings. "Brad, you're talking to the wrong one. I haven't been in town the last six years."

Cummings was working himself into a blind rage. "Shut up," he screamed. "Just your goddam name makes me sick. I'm giving you warning. Get out of town and stay out."

Gradie stared levelly at him. This damned old fool. Cummings was a greedy man when it came to revenge. Gradie had taken all he could. "And if I don't?" he asked silkily.

"Then I'll kick your ass out of town just like I did before," Cummings raged.

The memory of those humiliating moments burned Gradie's face brick-red. "If you're no smarter than that, you go ahead and try it."

Gradie's tone put a momentary hesitation in Cummings. Cummings wasn't too drunk to see the tenseness of Gradie's figure, the clenched hands, the burning eyes. He made a quick estimation of present values. He no longer faced a kid.

"By God, I'll do it," he said, but the bluster wasn't so pronounced in his voice.

"You aren't that stupid," Gradie said contemptuously. His laugh was a harsh, metallic sound. The sound weighed Cummings then tossed him aside as though not being worth further consideration.

Cummings's breathing was becoming labored. "Why, goddam you," he said, his words jerky and uneven. "I can get rid of you another way." He clawed for his gun, the movement slow and unco-ordinated.

"You damned, old fool," Gradie yelled. He had all the time in the world to beat this fumbling draw, but this was Letty's father.

Daugherty took a quick step as Cummings's hand moved. He grabbed the wrist before Cummings touched the gun butt.

"You don't want that, Brad," he murmured.

Daugherty whirled Cummings around and got his shoulder under Cummings's breastbone. He rammed him against the bar, smothering his struggles with sheer weight. Daugherty was a far more powerful man than Cummings. He held him easily with one hand, while he lifted Cummings's gun from his holster.

Daugherty let go of him then and tucked Cummings's gun in his waistband. "When you simmer down, Brad, you can have this back."

Cummings was livid with rage. He spit all over his chin, trying to get his words out, and his speech was unintelligible.

He managed to slow down and thrust his face close to Daugherty's. "That's going to cost you," he yelled. "You're going to be the sorriest man in this town."

Daugherty's face was blank. "I already am, Brad," he said wearily.

Gradie thought he would never have a better time to leave. He nodded his appreciation to Daugherty for his interference and started to step by Cummings.

Cummings's drinking and fury blended into a combination that wiped all sanity from his mind. He reached out, grabbed Gradie's arm and said, "I'm not through with you yet."

This was the second time Cummings had taken hold of him today, and it shattered the last of Gradie's restraint. He half pivoted and drove his fist into the biceps of Cummings's arm. The blow had power, for Cummings's face contorted under the pain.

"Don't make that mistake again," Gradie said coldly. His eyes raked Cummings, then he turned to continue on toward the door.

He heard the scrape of boots and Daugherty's shouted, "Gradie."

He whipped about, and Cummings was springing at him. Gradie grunted deep in his throat. This old man learned the hard way.

Gradie let his right fist fly. He held back nothing from this blow. He wanted to hurt Cummings and end this once and for all.

Cummings came in wide open, and Gradie's fist caught him on the hinge of his jaw. Cummings's face went slack, and his eyes were blank. He seemed to hang there for a long moment, then as his eyes rolled up into his head, he plunged forward on his face.

Daugherty turned him over with a boot toe. Cummings must have struck his nose against the floor, for he bled copiously.

Gradie met Daugherty's look and asked challengingly, "Well?"

Daugherty shook his head in weary resignation. "I don't see what else you could have done. I've never seen a man beg for it harder."

Gradie nodded. He swept the other three people in the room with a single glance and saw nothing that threatened him. He walked to the door and disappeared.

Gill breathed gustily. "There goes a man who's going to be damned sorry he hit Brad Cummings."

Disgust was written all over Daugherty's face. "Sometimes, Gill, I think you drink too much of your own whiskey." He tugged Cummings's pistol from his waistband and laid it on the bar.

"Give him this when he comes to," Daugherty said. He followed Gradie out of the door. He looked down the street after him, struggling with a decision. Daugherty shrugged. He couldn't do Gradie any good. Maybe it was best to drop the entire affair.

Water dropping on Cummings's face revived him. He spluttered, swiped at the water with one hand, and managed to sit up. He looked at his blood-stained shirt, and for a moment, it looked as though he was too foggy to understand what had happened.

Gill reached out with the wet rag again, and Cummings struck at the hand. "Get that away from me," he roared. "You trying to drown me?"

That injured Gill. "I was just trying to help, Brad. I wanted to—"

"When I need help, I'll ask for it," Cummings snarled. "That bastard swung on me when I wasn't looking." Those fierce eyes darted from face to face, daring anybody to disagree with his version.

"Sure, sure," Gill said hastily.

Cummings tried to rise and fell back. He swore in a steady stream. Gill bent over to help him, but Cummings struck at the proffered help. "Goddammit, get away from me. When I can't help myself, you'll hear about it."

The second attempt was successful, but Cummings was shaky on his feet. He threw out a hand to the bar to steady himself. His breathing came hard, and he was pale, but the fury still blazed from his eyes.

He stabbed a finger at each of the three in turn. "This ain't done yet." His voice rose higher and higher. "You hear me? I'm not through with that thieving Huston. Before it's over, he'll be damned glad to get out of Abilene as fast as he can."

He glared at all of them, then turned toward the door. His head jutted forward, as he thrust his boot heels against the floor.

The three men looked at each other, then shook their heads.

Cummings walked into Slaughter's office. Inman sat on the corner of Slaughter's desk, talking to the sheriff.

Slaughter's eyes widened at the blood on Cummings's shirt. "What happened to you, Brad?" he asked solicitously.

Cummings's face turned purple once again. "That bastard jumped me when I wasn't looking."

"Who?" Slaughter demanded. "I'll throw his ass in jail so quick his head'll spin."

Cummings bit down just in time to keep from saying Gradie Huston. There had been some witnesses to that little fracas. Cummings didn't know how Gill and the two customers would testify. He thought he could rely on them, but Daugherty was another matter. He was afraid Daugherty would tell it just the way it had happened. Cummings couldn't afford to be the laughingstock of the town. He'd better let that affair drop where it was. He made a savage chop with his hand. "Forget it," he rumbled. "I'll take care of that. But I want Gradie Huston run out of town."

Slaughter's eyes narrowed. "Was he the one—"

"Did I say he was?" Cummings shouted. "He's a damned Huston, isn't he? I don't want him hanging around. First thing I know, I'll be missing more stock. Run him out of town. I don't care how you do it."

Slaughter threw up his hands in a helpless gesture. "How am I going to do that? If he doesn't break any laws—"

Those mean, little eyes raked Slaughter. "Then you'd better find a way. You're the sheriff. You've got the power. Lean on him." He paused, then said significantly, "Or maybe the job's too big for you to handle. If it is, next month's selection can change that."

Slaughter shuddered. This old man had enough influence in this county to swing an election just about any way he wanted it to go.

"Brad," he said weakly, "you don't have to worry any more. I'll think of something."

"You'd better," Cummings said, and turned, and stalked toward the door.

Slaughter stared at the retreating figure. So Gradie Huston had busted Cummings one. He wished Gradie had knocked the old bastard's head off.

# CHAPTER ELEVEN

Gradie spent a pleasant hour talking to Tate Arnold. Two customers had interrupted that conversation, but otherwise Arnold's business was slow.

"Sure, I knew you all along," Arnold claimed when Gradie introduced himself. "I just didn't think you wanted to be recognized."

"The hell you did," Gradie said and grinned. "You felt like you should know me, but you couldn't come up with a name."

Arnold's truculence at being called wrong vanished, and he matched Gradie's grin. "Eyes ain't what they used to be," he confessed. "But I felt I should know you."

"You did that," Gradie conceded.

"I remember you well," Arnold reflected. "Always a serious-faced kid. You'd work your butt off all day long for a nickel."

"A nickel was a lot of money then," Gradie said soberly.

"I'm sorry about your family, Gradie."

"It's done," Gradie said harshly. It took a lot of little things to build up a moment, and when that moment was prepared, nothing could stop it from happening. He felt no resentment over Jude's and Phil's deaths, but Jonse's killing was a canker that kept eating on him. But he could understand how that happened. Jonse had pointed a rifle at Slaughter. Gradie would never forgive the sheriff, but morally and legally, Slaughter was guiltless.

"Hannah getting along all right?" Arnold asked.

"As well as could be expected, Tate." Gradie had just eaten supper with her, then had taken her back to the hotel. "She's worn out." He hadn't broached the subject of them leaving Abilene to Hannah. One look at her told him the timing was still wrong. But the time she needed to recover was pressing heavily on Gradie.

"She went through a lot," Arnold said sympathetically. He walked with Gradie to the door. "You let me know if there's anything I can do. Hannah's a good woman. She deserved better than she got."

Gradie appreciated Arnold's words, but he couldn't express his feeling. "I'll keep in touch with you, Tate," he said gruffly.

He glanced back after a few steps. Arnold stood in the doorway, watching him. Gradie was wrong about there not being another person in Abilene who'd lift their hand, if he needed help. Arnold made the second who wasn't against him. He grinned bleakly. Two still didn't stand up very well against an entire town.

He turned toward the livery stable. It would be completely dark in another ten minutes. Lights were coming on all along the street. He'd better untie Dog and let him run a little. His grin softened as he thought of how anxious Dog would be about him.

He hadn't taken a dozen steps when a woman's shrill voice rang out from across the street. "There he is," she said shrilly. "That's the one."

Gradie jerked his head toward the sound. Slaughter and Inman stood over there on either side of the woman. Gradie had a crawling feeling slither over his skin. He had the strong feeling that the three had waited for him to appear.

"Hold it, you," Slaughter bawled. He and Inman charged across the street toward Gradie, the woman following them.

Gradie's face went tight at the drawn guns in their hands, and his eyes were wary. He kept his right hand carefully away from his holster. He didn't know what this was all about, but that clammy feeling on his skin had increased.

Slaughter and Inman stopped on either side of him. Slaughter snapped, "You just be damned careful of what you do, Huston." He turned his head toward the woman. "You're sure this is the man, Flora?"

"Don't you think I'd know him again." Her voice had a tendency to break, and she sucked gulps of air. "Look what he did to my dress."

Gradie had never seen this woman in his life. She tried to stare back at him, and her eyes kept sliding away. One sleeve of her dress had been ripped at the shoulder, and it hung in tatters. She was a blowsy woman with the best years of her life behind her. Gradie had seen her type before. They could be found in any dance hall.

Gradie swung hot eyes toward Slaughter. "What the hell do you think you're doing?" he demanded angrily. This little commotion was drawing attention. People hurried down the street, drawn by the promise of excitement. Others looked out of store entrances and ran out to see what was going on. In a few more seconds, Gradie would be ringed about by people, and he had no doubt that their judgment would all be against him.

"You shut your mouth, Huston," Slaughter yelled. "Go on, Flora."

She broke off a sob and dabbed at her eyes. "I was just walking along when he grabbed me." she said. "He tried to drag me into an alley. I was lucky enough to break away from him. I ran, and he couldn't catch me." She raised her arm, displaying the ruined sleeve. "He did this." She was racked by a series of sobs. "You don't know how glad I was to see you, Sheriff. I knew I could point him out to you."

Gradie was so angry he could hardly speak. This was a blatant frameup. The guilt was apparent in the woman's shifty eyes. Slaughter and Inman weren't doing so well in concealing their triumph, either.

"How long ago was this supposed to happen?" Gradie demanded.

Flora licked her lips before she could answer. "Not over ten minutes ago," she said huskily.

"You're a liar," Gradie said coldly.

"You can't talk like that to me," she shrieked.

"I told you to keep your mouth shut," Slaughter roared. He nodded judiciously. "I'd say that time is about right, Flora. It was only a few minutes ago that you ran up to us, asking for help."

The crowd was growing, and a thin ring of people surrounded them. Slaughter had an audience, and he enjoyed it.

Slaughter raised his voice for the crowd's benefit. "You heard her. It's about time he gets taught how we feel about our decent women being bothered."

The murmur of indignation from the onlookers grew louder and more sustained. One of them called, "Maybe some time in jail will teach him something, Dent."

Satisfaction was apparent in Slaughter's nod. "Just what I had in mind. I'll show his kind that I intend to keep our streets safe for our womenfolk." He took a step toward Gradie, raising his gun. For an instant, it looked as though he intended slashing Gradie across the head with the barrel.

"We'll see how you talk after a few days in jail," he said grimly. He reached out to take hold of Gradie. "You're coming with me. I won't stand for any trouble from you," he warned.

"What's going on here?" The familiar voice came from behind the crowd.

Gradie blew out a sigh of relief as he saw Tate Arnold pushing his way through the ring of people.

"Slaughter just arrested me, Tate," he said. "He claims about ten minutes ago I tried to attack this woman. She says I tried to tear her clothes off."

Arnold snorted. "She's made a mistake, or she's a damned liar. You were in my store, talking to me. We musta talked a good hour."

The voices around Gradie broke out again, but this time the tone was changed. That was uncertainty in their voices. The people looked from Arnold to Slaughter, and their doubt grew.

"Tate, you don't know what you're talking about," Slaughter said furiously. "Or else you're claiming I'm lying."

Arnold leered at him. "Maybe you are, Dent. I wouldn't know about that. But everybody around here knows I'm not a liar."

All around him heads bobbed in solemn agreement.

Arnold's face was triumphant as he looked back at Slaughter. "I don't know what you're trying to pull, Slaughter. But between you and this woman, one of you is a liar. Maybe both." He bent forward to peer into Flora's face.

"Oh my God," he said in disgust. "Flora Martin. She left town a couple of years ago. She's gained some weight. Damn it, don't you people remember what she was?"

All eyes went to the woman. She squirmed uncomfortably, then said indignantly, "I don't have to stand here and take this."

"Tate's right," a man said. "That's Flora all right. I didn't recognize her until Arnold pointed her out." Laughter broke out as Flora shoved her way through the crowd.

Slaughter showed his misery. His eyes couldn't stay long on any face. "Looks like she's the liar all right," he mumbled. "Wonder why she tried to pull something like that."

"Maybe a better question would be to ask you why you did, Slaughter," Gradie drawled.

"Are you accusing me—" Slaughter tried to build up outrage in his voice and failed. He put away his gun and looked around at the faces again. "I don't know why she lied to me," he muttered. He shoved people aside to make a passage. He ducked his head as he walked, and Inman slunk along behind him. Neither of them looked around as a derisive laugh rang out.

"Don't you want me, Slaughter?" Gradie called.

Slaughter didn't answer. His boot heels beat against the walk.

Arnold took Gradie's arm and led him away.

"What do you suppose that was all about?" Gradie asked.

"Looks like you've got a bad enemy in town," Arnold observed. "Can you put a name to him?"

Gradie thought of Brad Cummings. Cummings was a vindictive man. He would never forgive Gradie for that blow. But it was hard to believe Cummings had a hand in what had just happened.

"Brad Cummings has no love for me," he said slowly. "But would Slaughter do this for him?"

"He would," Arnold said positively. "Everybody knows Slaughter is Cummings's man. Cummings put him into office." He peered anxiously at Gradie. "Don't take this lightly, Gradie. It looks like Brad's made up his mind one way or the other to get rid of you. You keep an eye open."

Gradie's grin was slow and twisted. "It looks like I have to, doesn't it?" he said reflectively.

# CHAPTER TWELVE

Cummings paced back and forth before Slaughter's desk. His face and jerky walk showed how furious he was. "Of all the goddam stupid things," he exploded. "This is the worst."

Slaughter stared sullenly at his desk. Inman wouldn't meet Cummings's eyes, either.

Slaughter tried to defend himself. "How did I know that Arnold would alibi him? I didn't know Huston had been in that store so long. It was that damned Flora—" He broke off to curse her.

"You stupid son-of-a-bitch," Cummings yelled. "Why in the hell did you pick a woman like her?"

Slaughter raised his hands and let them fall helplessly. "I saw her get off the stage. I was ready to run her out of town again when I thought she could be useful. I didn't think anybody would remember her."

"You stupid son-of-a-bitch," Cummings repeated. "I guess she worked cheap."

The sullenness returned to Slaughter's face. "I gave her five dollars to replace the dress she tore." He lifted his head, and his eyes flared. "Did you expect me to try and hire a decent woman?" He rushed on, trying to take that savage look off Cummings's face. "If I could've jailed Huston, he would have been glad to run when I let him out."

Cummings pulled a cigar from his pocket and jammed it into his mouth. He struck a match, his eyes never leaving Slaughter, while he got the cigar to drawing. "I didn't expect anything from you," he said in disgust. "From now on, I'll tell you what to do and how to do it."

Cummings knocked an ash off on Slaughter's desk. "I've got

89

it," he said with savage pleasure. "Huston hits me in the head and takes five hundred dollars off of me. I was too groggy to get a good look at him, but I think it was Huston."

Slaughter shook his head. "It won't work, Brad. How are you going to get him to do that?"

"Oh, for Christ sake," Cummings exploded. "All I have to do is to say he did it. You find the five hundred dollars in his room. You can arrest him then, can't you?"

Slaughter continued to shake his head. "How will the money get in Huston's room?"

"You damned idiot," Cummings snarled. "Do you know which end to put your pants on when you get up in the morning? You're going to plant it in his room. Then you find it later and arrest him."

Slaughter and Inman exchanged glances. "It might work," Slaughter said cautiously.

"It will work. It'd better," Cummings said ominously. "I'm going to the bank and get that five hundred dollars." He stomped out of the office.

Inman grinned at Slaughter. "You know, that old bastard's got a head on him."

"It ain't worked yet," Slaughter said gloomily.

Simmons was the desk clerk of the Drovers' Cottage when Slaughter and Inman walked into the lobby.

"Is Huston in?" Slaughter growled.

The clerk looked at the rack of pigeonholes. "No, he isn't. There's his key."

"Give it to me," Slaughter demanded.

Simmons was a slight man with owl eyes behind large glasses. His hand constantly rose to brush back the sandy hair that kept falling down into his face. Being around the law made him nervous. He was beginning to tremble now.

"I can't do that, Dent," he begged.

"Lot of clothing's been stole from Harmon's Emporium," Slaughter said easily. "I got a report Huston might be behind it.

I want to see if he's got any of that clothing in his room." He scowled at Simmons. "Or maybe you're in with him."

Simmons blanched. "Oh my God no," he moaned. He reached for the key and placed it in Slaughter's hand. He pulled at his fingers. "What will I do, if he comes in?"

"I won't be more than a couple of minutes," Slaughter said. "Just long enough to look around."

He turned and climbed the stairs, Inman following him. He unlocked the door and checked Inman as the deputy started to enter.

"You stay out here in the hall. Let me know, if somebody comes along."

Slaughter walked into the room, his eyes scanning the room. He pulled the brand-new five one-hundred-dollar bills out of his pocket. He hadn't held that much money before in his life. He walked over to a chest of drawers. He pulled out the top one, and his lips pursed. Huston had been buying a few new clothes. Slaughter rummaged through a new pair of pants, two new shirts, and several pairs of socks. This would be as good a place to hide the money as he could find. He placed the money under the shirts and pants, and rearranged them. He closed the drawer, pulled the door to behind him, and rejoined Inman.

"Didn't take you long," Inman observed.

"Long enough," Slaughter said and winked.

He walked back to the desk and handed Simmons the key. "Nothing so far," he said.

Simmons breathed a sigh of relief as he replaced the key. He was out of this.

Slaughter frowned at Simmons. "Don't you say anything about this to Huston. I still think he's got a hand in that robbery. I don't want you saying anything that will alert him."

"Not me," Simmons said fervently.

Dog readily broke to the rope. Gradie thought it best to keep him on the rope for a while. He didn't think there was any law against him keeping the dog, but he didn't know what might pop out of Slaughter's fertile mind. If somebody complained about

Dog running free, Slaughter could use that as a flimsy excuse to arrest Gradie.

He jerked Dog to a halt at the head of the block. Slaughter and Inman were just coming out of the Drovers' Cottage. There was something furtive in their manner. They seemed in a hurry to get away from the hotel.

"What do you suppose they were doing in there, Dog?" Gradie asked. His face darkened as he thought of Hannah. If those two had been pestering her, Gradie would take both of them apart.

He walked into the lobby, leading Dog. Something was bothering Simmons. He shook visibly, and his eyes were apprehensive.

"You shouldn't bring that dog in here," Simmons said in a weak voice.

"You ordering me to keep him out?" Gradie asked. "I'm just going to be here a couple of minutes."

"I guess it's all right then." Simmons looked distressed. That wasn't what he wanted to say.

Something was wrong. It was in Simmons's agitated manner, in the restlessness of his hands. Gradie could smell it like overripe carrion. He took the key Simmons handed him and bounced it in his hand.

"What did Slaughter and Inman want?"

Simmons made a faint noise that sounded like a squeak. He gulped, and his face paled. "I don't know what you mean," he stammered.

Gradie looked at the fine beads of sweat breaking out on Simmons's forehead. Simmons was trying to hide something and doing a miserable job of it. "You're lying," Gradie said evenly. "I saw them come out." His eyes bored into Simmons. Whatever purpose Slaughter and Inman had, it concerned him.

Dog sat on his haunches, eying Simmons.

"He's a funny dog," Gradie said in a conversational tone. "Lying always upsets him. Makes him madder than hell. You keep on lying, and I can't be sure of holding him. I'd hate to have him get loose and jump you."

Dog looked up at Gradie. Every tooth in his head showed. That was Dog's grin, but Simmons didn't know that.

Simmons briefly closed his eyes. "I don't know what you mean." His voice was little stronger than a whisper.

Gradie leaned forward as though to untie Dog. "He's got a sixth sense. He knows when I'm in trouble. Damnedest dog I ever had. He won't allow me to be hurt."

"Wait," Simmons squalled. The word was thick with terror.

"You'd be smart, if you told me what's bothering you," Gradie suggested.

"I didn't have anything to do with it," Simmons said wildly. "The sheriff wanted to look in your room. He claims somebody reported you stealing clothes from Harmon. He wanted to look. He was only up there a minute or two. He didn't find anything, Mr. Huston. Honest, he didn't."

"Ah," Gradie said thoughtfully. What did Slaughter want in his room? "I guess you better hadn't say anything to him about this little talk."

Sweat now ran down Simmons's face. "I won't," he babbled. "I promise."

Gradie jerked his head toward Dog. "You better hadn't."

Halfway up the stairs, he looked back at Simmons. Simmons looked as though he was going to faint.

Gradie unlocked the door and surveyed the room. It looked just the way he had left it. He tied Dog to the foot of the bed so Dog wouldn't bother him while he made a quick search. A board squeaked under his boot as he made a round of the room. He scowled at it. The end of the board was warped, putting pressure on the nails, until they were almost loose.

He finished his search, and he couldn't see anything that was out of place. His scowl grew. Slaughter had some reason for being up here. That crawling sensation on Gradie's skin increased. It screamed a warning at him, but he was too stupid to understand it.

He opened the top drawer of the chest. Nothing looked out of place here, either. As he pawed through the few articles of clothing, a flash of green caught his eye.

He lifted the shirts and pants, and five one-hundred-dollar bills lay there. There was his answer. There was no doubt that Slaughter would be back shortly to recover those bills. Gradie would be in serious trouble when that happened.

He took the bills out of the drawer and rearranged the clothing. Now a sense of urgency rode him. What would he do with this money? He didn't even consider stowing it in his pockets. That would be one of the first place Slaughter would look.

Gradie held the money a long moment, wracked by indecision. He considered under the mattress, then rejected the idea. That was another obvious place. He took several harried strides. He didn't even consider trying to carry the money out on his person. From now on, he was sure Slaughter would watch every move he made.

The board squealed again. Gradie's face brightened. Now, that was a place to consider.

Kneeling beside the warped board, he pulled a knife from his pocket. He opened the big blade and inserted it under the end of the board. He pried with extreme caution, fearing he would break the blade. The nails squealed a dismal protest as the pressure forced them up. When he finished, the board was raised above the remainder of the floor a good quarter of an inch. It was more than enough space to slip five bills out of sight. He fed the thin sheaf of bills under the board, forcing them as far back as he could. He straightened and put his boot on the board. Using all his weight, he forced it back into place. The board looked as it had before. He didn't dare stamp the board down, fearful that the noise would be heard downstairs. The board creaked in protest as Gradie walked back and forth a few times. He was afraid his prying had weakened the nails, but they looked as they were holding well enough.

He walked over and sat down beside Dog. "Best I can do, boy. Now we'll see what happens."

Dog gave him that lopsided grin.

"It ain't funny," Gradie grumbled. He would be sweating before this time was over. He thought he could expect Slaughter to be along now at any moment.

Composing himself the best he could, Gradie waited. It seemed an eternity passed, though he knew it was probably under ten minutes.

The hard hammering on the door jerked his head toward it. "This is it, Dog," he muttered. He raised his voice. "What do you want?"

"Open this door," a voice yelled. "This is the law."

"I didn't expect anybody else," Gradie muttered. He got up and opened the door. His face showed no emotion as he looked at Slaughter and Inman, but his armpits felt damp and sticky. Those two hadn't given him much time.

"What's this all about?" he demanded.

"You'll see," Slaughter said grimly. Inman had a covert grin on his face.

Slaughter shoved Gradie aside and strode into the room, Inman at his heels.

"You've got no reason to bust into a man's room this way," Gradie complained.

Slaughter fixed him with a baleful eye. "We'll see."

Dog growled at them, and Inman asked, "Shall I shoot him?"

"You stay away from him," Gradie snapped.

"You'd better keep him tied up, then," Inman blustered.

"Leave the dog alone," Slaughter ordered. He faced Gradie. "Brad Cummings was hit in the head and robbed not a half hour ago. He was carrying five hundred dollars. He didn't get a good look at who did it."

"But he's accusing me," Gradie said quietly.

Inman grinned at Slaughter. "He's a smart one, isn't he, Dent?"

"He thinks he is," Slaughter growled.

Slaughter made a quick and perfunctory search of the room. There weren't many places to look. He crossed the warped board a half-dozen times, and Gradie died inwardly each time the board squeaked.

Slaughter lifted the washbasin from the top of the chest of drawers and looked under it. By the mean look of satisfaction growing on Slaughter's face, Gradie could tell that the game was about over.

Slaughter opened the top drawer. He pawed through the clothing, and the blank look on his face was ludicrous. He swore furiously as he dumped the clothes onto the floor. His swearing increased as he pulled the drawer out and looked under it. Each drawer was pulled out and thrown onto the floor.

"Where is it?" he roared. "I know damned well you've got that money."

"You must be out of your head," Gradie drawled. "You didn't find it, did you?"

Slaughter cursed Gradie until he ran out of breath. The color congested in his face, and he looked as though he would choke. "Search him, Hebb," he finally managed to say.

"How about that dog?" Inman asked cautiously.

Gradie moved over to the far side of the room. "He won't bother you here," he said calmly.

The board squeaked under Inman's feet as he followed Gradie. Dog growled all the time Inman searched Gradie. The search was rough and thorough. Gradie had to undress, even to pulling off his boots. He stood in his underwear, his face composed.

Inman displayed the money he found in Gradie's pockets. "Less than forty dollars and some change."

"It sure isn't that five hundred dollars you talked about," Gradie said cheerfully.

Slaughter swelled up like a poisoned pup. "It's got to be in here," he insisted. "Strip that mattress off the bed."

Inman took a step toward the bed, then hesitated. Dog growled a warning. Inman made a decision, then shook his head. "Not with that dog tied there."

"If that's all that's bothering you," Gradie said. He padded in his sock feet to Dog and untied him. He led him away from the bed. Dog never stopped growling.

"Stop it, Dog," Gradie ordered. There was no real conviction in his voice, for Dog didn't listen to him.

Inman yanked the blankets and sheet off the bed. He pulled the mattress off, turned it over, then looked up at Slaughter with a negative shake of his head.

"Where did you put it?" Slaughter howled at Gradie.

The room was a shambles. "I'm getting sick and tired of this,"

Gradie said heatedly. "You come in and make accusations you can't prove. Get out of here. Now!"

Slaughter and Inman exchanged baffled looks, then trudged toward the door. There, Slaughter turned to throw Gradie a black look. "You ain't heard the last of this," he threatened.

"Get out of here," Gradie yelled. His display of anger was convincing, for they turned and hurried down the hall. He grinned weakly as he heard them arguing with each other all the way to the head of the stairs.

He closed the door and leaned against it. He wiped a hand across his face and wasn't surprised to find it damp. "Dog, they'll never know how close they were."

He redressed, his face thoughtful. This was the second time he had avoided a carefully laid trap. Luck wouldn't continue to run this way for him all the time. Cummings would try again. Cummings never let go of a grudge. The next time some trumped-up charge might stick. It was time for Gradie to get out of Abilene.

He put the mattress back on the bed and retied Dog. "I won't be long," he promised.

Hannah's room was on the floor above, and Gradie climbed the short flight of steps. He knocked on her door.

"You feeling any better, Ma?" he asked when she answered his knock. Her appearance answered his question. She didn't look any better. She looked so frail.

"Not much, Gradie," she said wanly. "I'm so tired. If I could stay here two or three days longer." She tried to smile, but it was a pitiful effort. "I guess it's been too long since I've really rested."

"Sure, Ma," he said gently. "I just wanted to see how you are. You go back and lie down."

His face was bleak as he went back down the stairs. That settled the question of leaving Abilene. He couldn't go until Hannah felt better.

# CHAPTER THIRTEEN

Cummings paced Slaughter's office like a caged animal. Everytime he passed the desk he smashed his fist down on it. Slaughter winced at each impact.

"I don't believe it," Cummings said for the dozenth time. "How could anybody be so damned stupid?"

Slaughter had the beaten look of a whipped dog. "I handled it just like you told me," he said sullenly. "The money wasn't in the room."

Cummings's face sharpened with a new look. His jaw thrust forward as he slowly looked Slaughter up and down. "It had to be, if you put it there. You claim you saw him go in and waited less than ten minutes before you followed him. He didn't leave the room, yet the money was gone. What happened to it?"

"You ask Inman if you don't believe me," Slaughter said hotly.

"All I want to know is what happened to my money?" Cummings's voice lowered several tones, and he almost purred. "Maybe it was never put in that room in the first place."

Slaughter had to struggle to digest that statement. His face paled, then crimsoned. "Are you saying—" He started shrilly.

"It was a lot of money," Cummings interrupted softly. "Split up between you two it would make a nice windfall."

Inman slouched in a chair. He had been content to let Slaughter take the brunt of the failure. But Cummings's remark put an entirely new air on the whole affair. Inman's head jerked up, and he blurted, "Now just a damned minute. If you're claiming—"

Cummings whirled on him. "Shut up," he howled. "Don't give me that righteous stuff. I only know my money is missing.

I want it back. I don't care how you get it, but I want it returned. If you two got it in your pockets, you'd better dig it out."

Slaughter got out of his chair. "I don't have to stand for this."

Cummings looked him over contemptuously. "You'll stand for anything I want to say." A crafty look crept over his face. "Maybe I wouldn't holler so loud about my money, if that worthless Huston was run out of town." He hesitated for emphasis. "Or dead. I'd prefer the latter. If that should happen, I'd feel it was money well spent." He strode to the door and turned there. "Think it over," he advised.

Inman waited until the echoes of Cummings's boot heels faded. "That old bastard ain't holding me responsible for his damned money," he said furiously. "It was all his idea in the first place."

Slaughter wanted to wring his hands. The election was coming up next month. Cummings's influence had put Slaughter behind the sheriff's badge the first time. Cummings would have the same amount of say-so in the next election. Slaughter almost groaned as he thought of being turned out of this office.

"We better take responsibility for that money," he said heavily. "Or next month, both of us will be out of jobs."

Inman stared at him, then swallowed hard. Slaughter meant that. Inman would hate to lose this job. The pay was fairly good, and the work wasn't arduous. Then there was always the hope of advancement, of wearing the sheriff's badge instead of a deputy's. Slaughter wouldn't last forever in this job. Whenever that happened, the people would naturally look to an experienced law officer to fill the void Slaughter left.

The thought of Cummings smashing everything, made him furious, but he kept his head. "Dent, what can we do?"

"I'm thinking," Slaughter said testily. He screwed up his face, but no logical thoughts came. All he could think of was that Huston had thwarted him twice. First, with that bitch Flora, then with the money. What had Huston done with that money? He had asked himself that question a hundred times, and hadn't come up with a sensible answer. Huston hadn't left the room.

Simmons verified that. That little mouse would be too scared not to tell the truth to him.

His head hurt with all this thinking. He opened a desk drawer and pulled out a bottle and two glasses.

Inman's eyes widened as Slaughter rubbed the glasses on his shirt sleeve. This whiskey was Slaughter's private stock. Inman had never known him to be generous with it before.

His eyes widened farther as Slaughter poured out the second drink for him. Damned if this wasn't a rare time. Neither of those drinks were skimpy.

"Maybe Brad had something," Slaughter said reflectively.

"What do you mean, Dent?"

"This town would be a better place, if we got rid of Huston. Wouldn't it?" he asked argumentatively. Inman's answer wasn't prompt enough to suit him. "He's made asses of the two of us. Does that please you?"

Inman scowled at him. "Hell no, but what do we do about it?"

Slaughter poured the third drink. "I say he needs shooting," he said reflectively.

The blunt statement startled Inman. But Slaughter could be right. Just the same he showed no indication of getting up and doing something about it. All he wanted to do was to sit here and talk about it. That suited Inman just fine. He would gladly sit here and jaw as long as the whiskey held out.

Dog whined as Gradie tied him in Eagle's stall again.

"It's for your own good," Gradie said as he roughed up Dog's ears. "Didn't you hear the deputy talk about shooting you? He's mean enough to do it. I'm trying to prevent that from happening."

From now on he'd have to keep Dog close. His eyes were moody as he contemplated the possibility of either Slaughter or Inman shooting Dog. They would have no real reason except pure cussedness.

Business was brisk in the Bull Head this evening. Maybe he would be smarter, if he chose another saloon, but it would probably be no different there. He was getting pretty well known all over town. Heads in another saloon would turn and stare at him just as they were doing in here.

He ordered a drink and carried it to an isolated table. One of the girls came up and asked, "Are you looking for company?"

"You're smart, if you're not," he said drily. "It could knock hell out of your popularity."

He grinned bleakly as she stared uncertainly at him. "I'm Gradie Huston," he said evenly.

Her eyes shifted nervously as she sought something to say. She looked toward the bar, and her face brightened at a nonexistent sign from one of the bartenders.

"Gill wants me," she said brightly. "Maybe I'll see you later."

"Maybe," Gradie said. He knew she wouldn't. She'd give him a wide berth from now on.

He ignored the curious stares that bombarded him. All he wanted was a little peace, but it didn't look as though he was going to get it in Abilene. Gradie stared moodily at the table top. He hoped that Hannah's recuperative powers were stronger than he thought they were. This town had been her home for so long he could understand her clinging to it, but he wanted her to make a stronger effort to cut those old bonds.

He made the drink last quite a while, then debated whether to buy another, or just get up and leave. But sitting here at this table won preference over sitting in that lonely hotel room. He shook his head at his miserable choice. He guessed he'd go up to the bar and order another drink.

Before he could rise, Cal Daugherty came into the saloon, his head turning as though he searched for somebody. He saw Gradie and hurried over to his table.

Daugherty's agitation showed in his eyes, in the tightness of his cheeks. "I've been looking all over for you," he blurted out.

"Why?"

"I think Slaughter and Inman are looking for you. A half hour ago I started to go into the office, and I heard Dent say it was about time to do something about the last Huston. He shut up when I came in. A bottle sitting between them was almost empty." Daugherty tried to grin. "Of course, I don't know how full it was when they started out."

Gradie's eyes narrowed. He had no idea of what Slaughter intended now, but it looked as though he was going to use a more direct method.

"Thanks, Cal," he said. "Get away from this table."

Daugherty opened his mouth to protest, and Gradie said savagely, "There's no use dragging you into this. I appreciate what you've done. It's enough."

Daugherty blew out a breath, nodded, then got to his feet. It looked as though he wanted to say something more, then he shook his head again, and walked up to the bar. He ordered his drink and kept watching Gradie in the back-bar mirror.

Gradie's black scowl grew. It looked as though they weren't going to leave him alone, he thought bleakly. I guess I spend the rest of the evening in that damned room. They made up my mind for me.

He half rose, then settled back into his chair as Slaughter and Inman came in. Maybe Daugherty's account had fed Gradie's imagination, but he could almost swear he saw a weave in Slaughter's walk. The two went straight up to the bar. Gradie thought cynically, if they're looking for me, they're not doing much of a job.

He waited until they ordered drinks. Both of them were engaged in conversation with the men on either side of them. Gradie had a small hope he could slip out unobserved. If he could, he might save a lot of trouble.

Gradie stood and walked toward the door. He thought he was going to make it when Slaughter bawled, "Hey, you. I want to talk to you."

Gradie briefly considered what he should do. He could keep on walking and reach the door in a few more strides, but that would be too much like running. He turned slowly, his face set; he would not run.

"What do you want?" he asked levelly.

Daugherty had called it right about this pair's drinking. Gradie could see the glaze in their eyes. He waited, feeling the tension creep slowly through him. There was no way of knowing which way they would push this.

Slaughter took a couple of unsteady steps toward Gradie and planted himself on widely braced legs. "I run an orderly town," he said thickly. "I don't allow anybody to upset that order."

"What are you looking for, a medal?" Gradie jeered.

Slaughter's face burned a bright red. "I won't take any of that wise talk," he warned. "You damned Hustons have been the scource of all the trouble around here. I ain't going to stand for it any longer."

"You took care of the other Hustons, didn't you, Slaughter? What are you complaining about? Nobody asked you any questions. You even shot a crippled kid who hardly knew what he was doing. That poor kid thought he was protecting his family. But you shot him down. Didn't that make enough of a hero of you? You make me puke, how the people of Abilene can stand you is beyond me." He shook his head, and the gesture was as scathing as his words. He looked Slaughter up and down, turned and continued on toward the door.

"Damn you," Slaughter bawled. "I warned you to get out of town."

"Gradie," Daugherty yelled. "Look out!"

Gradie reacted to the urgency in the voice, but not fast enough. A bullet sang past his ear as he whirled. His draw was completed before he finished his turn.

Slaughter shot at him the second time. His aim was better but not good enough. The second bullet plucked at the material of Gradie's shirt sleeve, and he felt a stinging there.

Gradie fired as his gun completed its swing toward Slaughter. The bullet smashed into Slaughter's shoulder, spinning him half around. He dropped his gun, a hand going to the shattered shoulder. His mouth was open as he sobbed in agony, and he weaved back and forth. He fought to retain his balance, then his legs buckled, dumping him heavily to the floor. Although his eyes were glazed, he wasn't unconscious, but he seemed unaware of what was going on.

Gradie whipped his gun toward Inman. Inman had no knowledge of what Slaughter had intended to do, or else he had reacted slowly, for he was just reaching for his gun.

"Touch it, and you're dead," Gradie said savagely.

Inman's hand froze a fraction of an inch above the gun butt, the rigid-splayed fingers looking like frozen claws. He looked at Gradie, then at Slaughter, then back to Gradie. An instinctive caution held his hand motionless. Then slowly he moved it carefully away from his side, licking his lips as he did so.

The tableau held for a long, frozen moment, then the babble of talk broke out, each person trying excitedly to give his version of what he saw.

Daugherty hurried up to Gradie, and there was no censure in his eyes. "You all saw it," he said loudly. "You saw Dent shoot at Huston."

Most of the heads bobbed in agreement. The gesture might have been reluctant, but there was no dissent in those faces. Several looked as though they wanted to yell protest, but a glance at Gradie still holding the gun weakened the desire.

Gradie's eyes bored into Inman. Inman was the ranking law now; his version was important.

Inman's eyes seemed riveted to the gun Gradie held, then they slowly lifted to Gradie's face. An unconscious tremor was in his hands. This Huston was about as fast with a gun as Inman had ever seen, and he hadn't lost his head, even with Slaughter firing at him.

"It was the way you say, Cal," he said haltingly. "I don't know why Dent lost his head—" Inman tried to grin.

Gradie's stomach felt strangely hollow as he put away his gun.

His eyes were cold as he looked down at Slaughter. The sheriff was moaning audibly now. Gradie knew the pain must be beginning to grip him like a relentless vise.

"Somebody better go get him a doctor," he said. Gradie looked at Daugherty. Daugherty had no doubt saved his life. Without that warning, Slaughter would certainly have had a chance for another shot. The third one might not have been as wide of the mark as the first two. Gradie couldn't say his thanks to Daugherty, not with all these people watching him. Daugherty would just have to sense Gradie's appreciation until Gradie got a better chance to say it.

"I'll be at the Drovers' Cottage, if you want me," Gradie said woodenly.

Daugherty nodded without speaking. Inman didn't say anything.

Gradie turned and walked out of the saloon. This time, nothing stopped him.

His departure released all the tongues in that room. Gradie could hear the buzz of their talk several strides beyond the doors. He wondered bleakly how much blame would be heaped upon him for this. But Daugherty had witnessed it all. This time, Gradie wouldn't have to worry about what would evolve out of this. Maybe this incident had swung a few more people to his viewpoint, but he couldn't count on it. Huston was still anything but a lovable name in Abilene.

He got his key from the desk and climbed the stairs. He unlocked the door and was vaguely aware of the squeaky board as he crossed the room. He thought of the money under that board and wondered if this latest encounter with Slaughter would stop the harassment. Sure, Inman had been in on the plan from the beginning, but Gradie didn't know if Inman had enough go-ahead in him to take over.

He sat down on the edge of the bed, his face bleak. Oh, he would hear from this and probably tonight. He could almost be sure of that. A crowd's viewpoint was a mercurial thing, swinging wildly in many directions under the slightest influence. Inman was there to talk against Gradie, and there might be more powerful voices to swing the crowd's opinion. A wry smile touched Gradie's lips as he thought of something. Cummings had missed a golden opportunity by not being there. He would have had much new fuel to add to his hatred, he could bellow his lungs out.

Gradie sat there a good half hour, his thoughts running first one way, then another. He couldn't find a solid spot on which to build. His thoughts were walking on quicksand. Each time they hesitated, they became mired down. He came up with the solution he had reached before. There was nothing for him in Abilene.

He lifted his head at the knock on the door. This was an ordinary knock with the usual polite request for admittance. It wasn't the insistent pounding Slaughter used.

Gradie opened the door, then stepped aside for Daugherty to enter. Daugherty carried a bottle.

"I thought this might come in handy," he said. "I know I could sure use a few belts."

Gradie looked about the room, and Daugherty sensed what he was seeking. "We don't need glasses, Gradie. If you never drank out of a bottle before, it's time you learned."

Gradie could almost grin freely. "I'm grateful to you, Cal. I'm—"

Daugherty stopped the words by thrusting the bottle at Gradie. "It's your bottle," Gradie insisted. "Go ahead."

Daugherty scowled at him. "If it's my bottle, I've got the right to say who drinks first."

Gradie took a long pull at the bottle before he handed it back to Daugherty. Daugherty was right. Gradie needed a drink.

Daugherty tilted the bottle up and said an appreciative, "Ah. I told that damned Gill he'd better give me good liquor."

Gradie sat down on the bed. This wasn't a luxurious room. There were no chairs. All he could offer Daugherty was a place beside him on the bed.

Daugherty sat down beside him. Each took another drink before he said, "How're you doing?"

"As well as can be expected," Gradie said gravely. Both of them had avoided the subject uppermost in their minds. Gradie plunged into it.

"How's Slaughter?"

"He's done," Daugherty said flatly. He made an impatient gesture at the tightening in Gradie's cheeks. "I don't mean that way. He'll live. But he'll do no more sheriffing. He's got a shattered right shoulder. Doc Barnes says it will never be any good."

Gradie was glad to hear that. Not from any remorse he might feel for Slaughter. But he didn't want any more trouble added to the burden he already carried.

"Quit blaming yourself," Daugherty said roughly. "He asked for everything he got. Hell, he asked for more. He's lucky to be alive."

"I wasn't blaming myself," Gradie said quietly. "How's the town taking it?"

Daugherty gestured vaguely. "Some feel like I do. Others are pretty unhappy about it. Inman isn't helping any. He keeps stirring things up."

Gradie's eyebrows rose, and Daugherty said, "This makes Inman a big man. He's acting sheriff; at least until next month's election. He wants to keep the town as unhappy about you as he can. It'll keep them from thinking about him. It looks like he's a pretty good politican."

"It does," Gradie said woodenly. Tomorrow, he thought, That's all I can give, Hannah. Then, we're leaving.

# CHAPTER FOURTEEN

Gradie paced the hall outside of Hannah's room while he waited for Dr. Barnes to make his examination. She looked so bad when Gradie had stopped by this morning to take her to breakfast, that he became alarmed. She insisted she wasn't hungry, and that increased Gradie's fears. He had hurried as fast as he could go after the doctor.

He paced the length of the hall, then turned and retraced his steps. He remembered Barnes well from the doctor's visits to the Huston soddy. Once, Gradie thought he was going to die and didn't even care. That was the sickest he had ever been in his life. Later, Hannah had told him he had had diphtheria. Dr. Barnes had quarantined the well the Hustons were using. How Jude had cussed at that. It meant he had to haul water from a much greater distance. Jude had given Gradie hell for the inconvenience. Dr. Barnes's visits to the soddy had not been frequent. The Hustons couldn't afford him. They usually toughed out whatever sickness hit them.

Gradie stopped before Hannah's door and looked anxiously at it. Damn, it was taking Dr. Barnes so long. An idle thought flashed through his mind. He wondered if Barnes had been paid for those few visits he had made to the soddy. He would have to ask about that.

The door opened, and Barnes came slowly out of the room. The years were bearing heavily on Barnes now. His shoulders were stooped, and the youthful carriage was gone. His face was seamed, and the skin of his throat hung in ever-thickening folds. The eyes were fading, but they could still call up a fiery spark.

109

"How is she?" Gradie demanded.

"She's completely exhausted," Barnes said with asperity. "That's mainly her trouble. She's been going on nerves for too long. I've prescribed a tonic for her, but she isn't young any more. She's not going to bounce back right away. What's she's been through recently demanded a heavy toll. She's going to need a long rest."

Gradie's heart sank. He knew what Barnes's answer would be, but he asked anyway. "Then she's not able to travel, even if we take it in short stages."

Barnes's snort was an eloquent answer. Gradie fell into step with him. Things were pressing in harder around him. He wasn't broke, but two rooms and food was a steady and considerable drain. He thought of Dog with wry humor. There were three mouths to feed.

Barnes had a perceptive mind. "You worried about money?"

"Some," Gradie admitted. "I will be, if I sit around here much longer. I've got to find a job." He shrugged. "I don't even know where to start looking."

Barnes's question about money reminded Gradie that this visit wasn't paid for. He reached into his pocket and pulled out some bills. "How much do I owe you, Doc?"

"Let it go," Barnes said brusquely.

That stubborn cast set on Gradie's face. "No. And I know there's some back bills the Hustons built up. I want to take care of them too."

Those sharp, old eyes inspected Gradie. "You owe me a dollar. The old bills were taken care of."

Gradie looked helplessly at him. He couldn't call Doc a liar, but he felt he was lying.

Barnes took a dollar, folded it and stuck it into his pocket. "I'll be back tomorrow to see how Hannah's doing."

"I'd be grateful." Gradie stopped Barnes before he started away. "How's Slaughter?"

Again, those speculative eyes weighed Gradie. "He's going to make it. But he'll never be able to use that shoulder much."

Gradie felt obliged to defend his position. "I didn't want that to happen," he said slowly. "But—"

"I know," Barnes interrupted him. "It upsets a man considerably to have another shoot at him."

Gradie's face cleared. "Then you got the straight of what happened."

"I got it," Barnes said drily. "I was there a few minutes after it happened. That's when it's most likely for the truth to come out. Give people some time to think it over, and they begin to twist things around. If it suits their need, they'll go to the extent of making up lies."

The dark, brooding look returned to Gradie's face. "I know. I'm experiencing some of that."

Barnes let a reassuring hand rest briefly on Gradie's shoulder. "Quit fretting about it. Just do what you have to do. Usually, it turns out right." He stepped out of the hotel and plodded on down the street.

Gradie stood in the doorway, watching him go. Doc Barnes was a crusty old codger, but he was fair and honest. Gradie could put another name on the list of those he could be absolutely sure weren't against him.

He sighed and turned toward the livery stable. It was time to take Dog out for his morning run. Since Inman's remark about shooting Dog in Gradie's room, Gradie hadn't dared let him run free without keeping a close eye on him. By now, Dog would be hungry too. Gradie made a wry face. Dog was a bottomless pit.

Gradie had an arrangement with Sawyer at the stable. He gave Sawyer two-bits a day for all the scraps he could gather up for Dog. Sawyer made a daily round of the restaurants, gathering up the scraps. Sawyer knew better than to try to palm off an old bone on Dog and still claim his quarter. Gradie expected a generous amount of scraps in exchange for the quarter. It had to be to keep Dog satisfied.

He walked into the stable, and Sawyer handed him a sack. Gradie hefted the sack and nodded. The amount in the sack ought to satisfy even Dog. Sawyer refused to feed Dog, claiming he was fearful that Dog might not be able to differentiate between the scraps and his arm.

Gradie handed Sawyer the quarter. It was a small sum, but it was a steady drain on his dwindling resources. He couldn't help but think of the five hundred dollars under the board in his room. He thought ruefully, it's getting harder to keep telling myself that money's not mine.

Sawyer stood with Gradie and watched Dog gulp down the scraps. "He kinda grows on you," he said grudgingly. "I couldn't stand him at first. That ugly ole cuss kinda gets to you, doesn't he?"

"Something like that," Gradie said with a slight grin. He wouldn't have to wait very long for Dog to finish his meal. Dog didn't fool around when it came to eating.

Gradie adjusted the rope around Dog's neck. Just Dog's presence kept the curious a good distance from Gradie. Gradie didn't have to listen to their veiled remarks over the sheriff's shooting.

"Let's go, boy," he said. Dog made his walking easier. All he had to do was to lean back on the rope and let Dog drag him along.

Letty was just getting out of her buckboard in front of Arnold's store as Gradie turned the corner. He was tempted to turn back the other way, but Letty had already seen him. Gradie was both glad and sorry to see her again. He didn't know what distorted story she had of the incident in the saloon.

She wasn't afraid of Dog. She took his head between her hands and gently shook it. That put Dog in ecstasy. He tried to lick her hands as he wriggled all over.

"He gets prettier every time I see him," she said and laughed.

Gradie nodded soberly. Letty didn't treat him as though he had some loathsome disease. "I kinda like him," he confessed. He hesitated a moment, then plunged into the subject that had to be on both of their minds. "I guess you heard about last night."

"Yes," she said honestly. She searched his face, and there was concern in her eyes.

"I guess you've heard different versions of how it happened," he said doggedly.

"Yes," she said frankly. "But I also talked to Cal earlier this morning."

Gradie felt all loose and good inside. She knew exactly how it had happened.

"Gradie, why was the sheriff so determined to run you out of town?"

He shrugged. "Just a nutty notion he had in his head."

"Did my father have something to do with it?"

Everything, he thought violently, but held back the words. "I don't know."

She wasn't satisfied with his answer. "I asked him about it. Did you know that he lost five hundred dollars in a robbery?"

"I heard something about it," he admitted.

"He thinks it could have been you. He can't swear to it. It happened so quick that he didn't get a look at who did it." Those candid eyes searched his face.

Gradie wanted to say, he's lying. Instead, he said, "He's wrong, Letty."

"I knew it," she said and sighed.

He wanted to tell her about the money under the board and hand it over to her. But he couldn't do that yet. It was Cummings's money all right. But giving it back now could put doubts in her mind. He knew how Brad Cummings would take such a gesture. He would bellow triumphantly, "I knew it all the time." The money would have to stay where it was until a more propitious time.

"I'm glad, Gradie," she said softly. "How's Hannah?"

Gradie frowned. "Not as well as I'd like. Doc Barnes says she's completely exhausted. I guess she needs a long rest."

Her face was expressive; it showed how she felt about everything. "Is there anything I can do, Gradie?"

He shook his head. "Not that I can think of now. I'll let you know, if there is."

"Good." She lightly touched his forearm. "I've got to rush. I promised the church I'd bake two pies for the pie supper tonight. Are you coming?"

Her eyes begged him to say yes. He regretfully shook his head.

"I'd like to Letty. But other things—" He gestured vaguely and let the sentence die.

"I'm sorry," she replied and hurried into Arnold's store.

Gradie stood there a long moment, looking after her. She meant that. He wanted to curse at his helplessness. But if he appeared at that pie supper, the people there could give him a hard time. And her, too, he thought gloomily. That didn't include Cummings's being there. Cummings would tear the roof of that church, if and when he saw Gradie.

Gradie wanted to swear. Circumstances had a way of tying a man's hands, and he could do nothing about it.

"Come on, Dog," he said and sighed. That momentary brightness at the sight of Letty was completely gone.


Inman was in a fine mood this morning. He had put on Slaughter's badge; and who had a better right to wear it? Slaughter was never going to come back. That was common knowledge. Inman had walked about town, and he hadn't found anybody who objected to his wearing the badge. Everybody said they knew he would do a good job. To each one he had modestly proclaimed, he would do the best he could.

He stopped to talk to Wilbur Haines, who was moving some crated merchandise from the walk into his hardware store. Some of those boxes looked heavy.

"Let me give you a hand with that, Wilbur," Inman said.

His struggles with the merchandise had turned Haines's face red and shortened his breath. He didn't have too much heft, and age was beginning to encroach on him.

"Be grateful, Hebb," he said. "Damned boxes get heavier every year."

"Ain't it the truth," Inman said and grinned. "Let me have that one."

He picked up the box and carried it into the store and grunted as he set it down. He would bet that one would go close to a hundred pounds. One of these days and soon, Haines was going to have to hire some muscle.

Inman helped Haines clear the sidewalk and leaned against a counter mopping his face. "Old sun's bearing down, ain't it?"

"It sure is," Haines said fervently. "Can't tell you how grateful I am, Hebb."

Inman felt a smug satisfaction. He had sure tied up Haines's good-will. It would show up in next month's election.

Haines's eyes rested on the badge Inman wore. "You figuring on taking over that badge permanently?"

"That depends upon how the voters look at it," Inman said modestly.

"By God, you deserve it. Have you heard how Dent is?"

"Stopped by to see him this morning. He ain't going to be worth a damn any more. Damned shame. Dent was a good sheriff." Inman's face clouded. "I'm kinda blaming myself. I might have saved Dent that."

Haines's eyes widened. "What could you do about it? The way I heard—"

"You heard wrong," Inman said evenly. "I was there and saw it all. That Huston badgered Dent until he couldn't stand it any longer. Oh, I'll admit Dent might have lost his head. But under the circumstances, anybody else would have." Inman woefully shook his head. "I never saw a slicker hand with a gun than that Huston."

"But I heard Slaughter fired first," Haines protested.

"It wasn't that way," Inman said firmly. "Huston kept deviling Dent until he went for his gun. That was what Huston wanted. Dent didn't have a chance. I'm surprised he's still alive. I'll admit I was too slow to help him. Huston had me covered before I could touch my gun. I swear I never looked into worse killer eyes. That Huston wanted me to make the same mistake Dent did. He wanted me to draw on him." He shook his head apologetically. "But I didn't see where it'd do any good to get myself killed or shot up like Dent is."

"That damned Huston," Haines said explosively. "He's like his family. They've never been nothing but trash. This town will be better off when the last one is run out."

"My sentiments, Wilbur. I'm working on it. Believe me, I'm

keeping an eye on him. The first wrong move—" He let expressive gesture finish for him.

Haines walked with Inman to the door. "You know everybody is behind you, Hebb."

"You don't know how much that bucks up a man. Be seeing you, Wilbur."

He strolled down the street, keeping the scorn he felt off his face. People were a damned stupid bunch of sheep. Just point them the way you wanted them to go, then you'd better get out of the way before they ran over you. He whistled a tune as he walked. Things couldn't be going better.

Letty was coming out of Arnold's as Inman approached. Her arms were laden with packages.

Inman sprang forward. "Here now. Let me give you a hand with that. Girl like you should never be turned into a pack mule."

That pulled a slight smile from her. "Then you think I look like a pack mule now."

"Aw, now," he protested. "You know I didn't mean anything like that." He felt pleasantly warm all over. This was the first time she had ever responded to him in any way. She had always intrigued him, but he never had been able to dent that cool, standoffish manner. It emboldened him to ask, "Are you going to the pie supper."

She laughed. "I'm afraid I am. I promised I'd bake two pies. I'd better get started, or I'll never make it."

Inman deposited the packages in the buckboard. He hadn't yet asked her to go with him, but her manner encouraged him. "Maybe we could go together," he suggested.

"Oh, I'm sorry," she exclaimed. She sounded as though she meant that. "Maybe some other time."

He didn't feel too letdown. She hadn't actually said no, and she did look sorry. He had just asked her too late.

"I'm sorry, too," he said and grinned. "Maybe I'll see you there tonight."

She seemed to hesitate before she said, "That would be fine,

Hebb." This time, her pause was definitely noticeable. "I'm sorry to hear what happened last night."

He wished he could read her thoughts. But she was Brad Cummings's daughter, wasn't she? She would have the same feelings.

"Bad thing," he said gravely. He repeated the same story he told Haines. "That Huston didn't give poor ole Dent much of a chance. If I ever saw a killer, Huston is one."

She hid her thoughts well. He couldn't read a thing in her face.

"It's bad, Hebb."

Was that a hollow ring to her words? Inman couldn't be sure.

He helped her into the buckboard. "I'll look forward to seeing you tonight."

She lifted the reins. "That'll be fine, Hebb."

Inman watched her drive away. He wanted to whoop with elation. This was his time. Everything was going his way.

# CHAPTER FIFTEEN

Cummings slapped the reins on the mare's rump to get an ounce more speed out of her. The buckboard lurched as it ran over a rock in the road.

"Papa," Letty cried sharply. "My pies. I don't want to get to the church with them all broken."

"These damned church affairs are a pain in my—" Cummings hastily amended what he intended to say. "In my neck."

"You won't go then?" she asked.

"I told you I wouldn't," he said testily. "I got some things to do around town. I'll pick you up after it's over."

Cummings kept glancing at his daughter as he drove. Something was bothering her. All day, she had barely spoken to him. When she was displeased with him, she pulled in like a disturbed turtle, and he couldn't pry open her shell.

The silence between them held while he drove another mile. He raged inwardly. Not at her, but at that bumbling Slaughter. All Slaughter had accomplished was getting himself shot up, and the five hundred dollars was still missing. Cummings had decided that Gradie Huston had that money. Huston had been able to outsmart Slaughter as easily as he had been able to outshoot him. Just thinking about it made him furious. Slaughter was out of it, but that only transferred the responsibility of getting that money back to Inman. He'll get it for me, Cummings thought darkly, or Inman wouldn't be in that office very long. Letty's silence broke him down, and he begged, "Say it, Letty."

"You blame Gradie for shooting Dent Slaughter, don't you?" she asked coldly.

So that was what was bothering her. "Why shouldn't I?" he

said heatedly. "I know he's the one who stole my money. When Dent tried to arrest him, Huston shot him."

She stared straight ahead. "Other people tell it differently." Her voice was devoid of all feeling.

"Who tells it differently?" he demanded. He could feel sweat beginning to trickle down his sides. Letty had more determination than was good for a woman. When she got hold of an idea, she never let go.

"Gradie did, for one," she said evenly.

"You've been talking to him," he accused.

The impact of her eyes was like a club. "Don't start that again, Papa. You can't stop me from talking to whom I please."

She meant that. His authority over her was gone. If he laid down his rockbound rules as in the old days, she would leave him.

"You'd believe him before you'd believe your father." He let his injury show in his voice.

"Maybe under the circumstances I should," she said wearily.

He was glad he was almost to the church. If this kept up much longer, he would be yelling at her. Then she wouldn't speak to him for sure.

"What circumstances are you talking about?" He tried to keep his voice calm.

"You did kill Gradie's father and brothers."

Cummings's indignation almost choked him. Good God, couldn't she see where he had every right to protect his own property? What did she expect him to do, take the Hustons's stealing until he was robbed blind. "By God, don't you think I had the right to do what I did?"

A faint shudder ran through her. "Does that include Jonse too?"

The unfairness of her question struck him speechless. Slaughter was the one who had killed Jonse, and Cummings couldn't be blamed for that. "You only see it through the eyes of trash," he said bitterly.

There was a sad knowledge in her eyes as she looked at him. "You really hate him, don't you, Papa? I don't believe Gradie had anything to do with stealing your money. Maybe you only used that story to send Slaughter out to shoot him."

Cummings's mouth dropped open. The accuracy of her guesses shook him. He was glad when he pulled up before the church. He was hurt and furious and a little scared. If he didn't get the poison out of her mind, he could readily lose her.

Without looking at her he asked, "What time do you want me to pick you up?"

She didn't look at him, either. "It should be over at nine."

The coldness in her voice scared him. The rift between them was steadily widening. He hadn't convinced her of anything. His stomach churned, and his hatred of Gradie Huston knew no bounds.

"I'll be back for you at nine," he said thickly.

Letty stepped down from the buckboard without answering him. Her back was stiff, her shoulders square as she walked away. A dismal little thought ran through his mind. Maybe it was too late to run Gradie Huston out of town; maybe he had already lost Letty.

He lashed the mare into a full run. He whipped around a corner, the buckboard tilting far over on two wheels.

Sweat popped out on his forehead as he realized how close he had come to overturning the buckboard. He slowed the mare down. Driving around blind wasn't going to solve anything, and it could readily get him a broken neck. Instead of raving and cussing, he better start thinking again. He wouldn't rest peacefully until two things happened; he got his money back and Gradie Huston was run out of the way.

Cummings drove up before the sheriff's office and climbed down. The old aches seemed intensified tonight. Getting old, he thought. Somehow that thought frightened him for the first time. He shook his head angrily as he walked into the office. Why was he getting these crazy thoughts recently?

Cal Daugherty sat behind the desk. He nodded and said, "Evening, Brad."

Cummings had never made up his mind about Daugherty. Slaughter had hired him without conferring with Cummings, and his initial irritation at the new deputy had never completely vanished. Daugherty had a trick of looking at him as though he was weighing him. Cummings snorted. There was another one of those crazy thoughts. It was ridiculous to think that some twobit deputy was weighing him.

"Where's Inman?" he asked.

"Out."

The shortness of the answer angered Cummings. To get any sensible reply out of this deputy, Cummings had to pull a word at a time out of him.

"Dammit. I can see he isn't here. Where is he?"

Again, those veiled eyes weighed Cummings. Daugherty shrugged. "He didn't say where he was going."

Cummings glared at Daugherty. If Inman expected to run successfully for sheriff in the next election, he had better pick himself a new deputy.

Cummings started to stamp out of the office, then reconsidered. He wanted some information. "How does the town feel about Dent's shooting?"

The color rose in Cummings's face at the length of time it took Daugherty to answer.

"Some see it one way; others another," Daugherty said slowly.

The color grew higher in Cummings's face. "You were there. How do you see it?"

"I hate to see a man shot," Daugherty said gravely.

The oath almost slipped out of Cummings's mouth. He wasn't going to get anything out of this bastard.

He whirled, and his boot heels rang angrily against the floor as he left the office. His mind was made up. Inman wouldn't get his backing unless he fired that tight-mouthed deputy.

He drove around town, hoping to see Inman on the streets. His rage steadily mounted. Inman was probably with some floozie he picked up out of one of the saloons. Inman wasn't fit to wear the sheriff's badge.

Cummings tied the mare to a hitching rack and walked into the Easy Aces Saloon. He curtly returned the bartender's greeting and ordered a bottle. The brooding expression on his face kept the man from pushing a conversation with him. He took his bottle and walked to a table and sat down. His expression said he didn't want anyone to bother him. The only one he wanted to talk to was Hebb Inman.

He drank slowly but steadily. The level in the bottle lowered, but his thoughts were still crystal clear. He lurched as he stood. There was still a half hour before he went after Letty, but he hoped she had grown tired of that affair and was ready to leave early. He didn't untie the mare. The church was only a block away, and he needed the walk.

As Cummings turned the corner, he saw Inman and Letty out in front of the church. Cummings stopped in the shadow of a bush, and his eyes glittered. Inman must have said something that amused her, for Letty laughed. Cummings boiled. So that was where Inman had been; with Letty. Cummings had to lay out several things that Inman would have to get clear in his thick head.

Letty turned and went back into the church. Inman stayed to light a cigarette. Inman would probably stay out here long enough to finish the smoke before he followed her.

Cummings hurried up to him.

Inman missed the black look on his face, or ignored it.

"Hello, Brad," Inman said easily. "Hot in the church." He pulled on the cigarette and blew out the smoke. He seemed very satisfied with himself. "Letty wanted a breath of air."

"I want to talk to you," Cummings said. He had trouble in getting out the words without running them together.

Cummings's tone put a tightness in Inman's face. "Sure, Brad," he answered, but the easiness was gone from his voice.

"Not here," Cummings said. He doubted he could talk to this man without raising his voice. That could pull curious people out of the church. If Letty heard, it would only disturb her more.

Cummings started off down the darkened street, looking back over his shoulder to be sure that Inman followed him.

Inman lengthened his stride to catch up. "You're sure in a sweat about something, Brad." He said it mildly enough, but there was a new watchfulness in his eyes.

All of Cummings's pent-up temper broke. "You're goddam right I am. What makes you think you got a right to talk to Letty any time you want to?"

Inman's nostrils pinched together with the rush of his breathing. "Are you ordering me not to talk to her?" His eyes grew narrow and mean. "Maybe you don't think I'm good enough to talk to her."

"You're beginning to get the idea," Cummings said sarcastically.

Inman blew out a hard breath. "Just a damned minute," he said hotly. "When can't a sheriff talk to anybody he wants to?"

Cummings's sarcasm deepened. "Oh, I forgot. You think you're no longer a deputy. You think wearing that badge is permanent. That makes you an important man, doesn't it? It'll bring you all of fifty dollars more a month."

Cummings stabbed a forefinger into Inman's face. "You won't even be a deputy, if you can't get two things straight in your head. Stay away from Letty and find my five hundred dollars. You think I'm just making noise? Fail on either one of those things and see how long you last. Hell, I'll see to it that your name don't even go on the ballot."

Fury rose up in Inman's throat. The sickening part of it all was that Cummings could do exactly what he said. Inman shook with impotent rage. Just when he was so positive that everything was going his way, this old bastard came along and spoiled it all. Inman could do one of the two things; he could be sure he stayed well clear of Letty. But he could do nothing about that missing money. He and Slaughter had thoroughly searched Huston's room. The money wasn't there, unless—Inman's eyes went round at a sudden thought. Unless it had never been there in the first place. He hadn't been with Slaughter when Slaughter was supposed to have placed the money in the room. Why, Dent could have stuck Cummings's money in his pocket. If he did, he had gotten himself pretty well shot up for it. Inman knew a sense of wicked satisfaction, but it didn't last long. Cummings was blaming him for what Slaughter did. By God, Inman had no intenton of taking the blame.

"You remember what I said," Cummings said. He whirled and took three strides on down the street.

Inman quickly looked around. They had covered a good two blocks from the church. None of the nearby houses were lighted, and this spot was lonely and dark.

"Brad," Inman said softly.

The words were loud enough to reach Cummings. He stopped but before he could turn, a bullet tore into his spine. He came apart all at once and fell as though there wasn't a whole bone in his body.

Inman put away his gun, the savagery still in his eyes. "You were an old bastard," he muttered. "You won't be ordering anybody around any more."

He jerked his head about as he heard a cry, dimmed by distance. That shot had been heard. He pounded down the street toward an alley a half block ahead.

# CHAPTER SIXTEEN

Daugherty found Inman at the far south end of town. "I've been looking all over for you."

"And now you've found me," Inman drawled. "What's eating on you?" He hoped he sounded easy and undisturbed. Inside, his guts hurt from the tension.

"Cummings's been shot," Daugherty announced abruptly.

"Naw," Inman said in convincing disbelief.

Daugherty nodded. "Shot in the back. About two blocks from the Baptist church."

"How bad?" The proper concern was in Inman's tone. He knew how bad it was.

"Dead," Daugherty said. "He's at Compton's."

Inman swore softly. "Shot in the back? Who had it in for Brad that much? Huston?"

"Brad was a hard man," Daugherty said matter-of-factly. "He made many enemies."

Inman writhed inwardly. Daugherty's answer didn't tell him very much; it didn't tell where suspicion was directed. He swore at himself. Daugherty would never suspect him.

"Does Letty know about this?"

"She's at Compton's. Thought I'd better look you up. Damn," Daugherty grumbled. "Thought I'd never find you."

"We'd better get over there and see how she's doing," Inman said decisively.

Daugherty wanted to set off at a run. Inman checked him. "Saving a minute or two ain't going to help Brad."

Daugherty flushed at the implied criticism. Inman kept his face blank. Daugherty felt the heat crawling up into his face.

This was his first murder case, and he was running around like a chicken with its head off. His mouth thinned as he fell in with Inman's pace.

"Talked to anybody yet?" Inman asked. "Anybody got an idea?"

Daugherty shook his head. "Didn't take time to talk to anybody. Quite a few had gathered before Compton's when I left. They're—" He paused, hunting for the word he wanted.

"Upset?" Inman finished for him. At Daugherty's nod, he said. "People always are upset by a murder." He rechecked his actions after he shot Cummings. The street had been dark, and he hadn't seen a soul. But there was always the off chance that somebody had seen him running away from the scene. He scoffed at the worry as he glanced covertly at Daugherty. He was almost positive that nobody had been around. If anyone had seen him, it would surely have been reported by now. His guts still hurt. The tension wouldn't let go of him. He would just have to wait and see how things developed.

A group of two dozen people was gathered before Compton's door. They crowded around Inman and Daugherty, throwing questions so fast that Inman couldn't begin to keep up with them.

"Whoa," he said. "One at a time. Anybody around when it happened?" The negative shakes of their heads reassured him. If anybody had any pertinent information, they would have volunteered it by now. Daugherty had called it right when he said Brad Cummings was a rough man. Inman had no doubt that every person here at some time or another had been offended by Cummings's harsh manner. But they were indignant now. Murder had a way of sweeping aside all past injured feelings.

"You got any idea who did it, Hebb?" Haines asked.

"Maybe I have, and maybe I haven't," Inman drawled. "We'll take it a step at a time and see what happens." He pushed through the crowd and entered Compton's, Daugherty at his heels.

Compton was talking to Letty. Her face was drawn and pale, and her hands were clenched too tightly.

Inman went up to her and took one of her hands. He gently forced it open. "I don't have to tell you how sorry I am, Letty. Is there something I can do?"

She shook her head. Right now, her thoughts were so jumbled up that she couldn't get a hold of a clear one.

Her eyes were dull and unseeing. She tried to speak, and a sob broke up her words. She shut her eyes. When she reopened them, her words came clearly enough.

"I don't know who it was who ran in and told everybody at the church about finding Brad. I looked for you, Hebb. But you were gone."

Inman swore inwardly. That placed him near the scene. Had Daugherty caught that? If so, nothing showed on his face.

"I had to make a round of the town, Letty," Inman said easily. "I wish to God that I had been there. Though I doubt if I could have done anything to save Brad. Can I take you home?"

She shook her head. She looked lost and lonely. "Not now," she whispered. "I want to stay here a little longer."

He pressed her hand. "Sure," he said softly. "I'll be around, if you need anything."

He looked at Compton and said fiercely, "You see that she gets whatever she wants."

"You know I will," Compton assured him.

Inman beckoned for Daugherty to follow him and walked outside. The group of people before the building had grown.

"How's she taking it, Hebb?" Haines asked.

"Hard," Inman said gravely.

"Goddammit," Haines said passionately. "I hope you get whoever did it. A damned backshooter!"

Inman's face was sober. "I intend to." His eyes gleamed as a thought flashed into his mind. He might be able to lay his hands on a killer who would satisfy the entire town. If he could accomplish that, it would close the matter of Cummings's death once and for all.

He pushed through the cluster of people and waited for Daugherty to join him. "I want to find out where Huston was," he said in a hard voice.

"You don't think—" He couldn't finish the sentence.

"That's what I'm going to find out," Inman replied. "Can you think of anybody more suited to fill the bill right now? Damn it," he said at the stubbornness settling over Daugherty's face, "who would have more reason? After what Brad did to his family? To add to that, Huston and Cummings had a row the other night. Huston knocked Brad down. Maybe that wasn't enough to satisfy Huston."

Daugherty kept shaking his head, and Inman exploded, "Goddammit, I'm going to look into it."

A smug satisfaction filled Inman as they walked toward the Drovers' Cottage. He didn't give a damn what Daugherty thought. The town was ready to believe that Huston could be Cummings's killer. Inman had talked to enough of them to know how they felt about Huston.

Daugherty hadn't spoken a word most of the way here. To hell with him, Inman thought. After he was elected sheriff, maybe he better get himself a new deputy. The thought gave him satisfaction. Daugherty was out, though he might not know it.

Simmons was behind the desk, and that harried expression came back to his face as Inman and Daugherty walked up to him. Inman grinned cynically. Simmons was always nervous when the law came around.

"Huston in his room?" Inman asked.

"He is," Simmons replied. He couldn't keep his hands from trembling, and he took them off the desktop.

"How long ago did he come in?"

"Maybe forty-five minutes ago. Under an hour any way."

Inman's hard eyes bored into him. "How'd he look?"

"I don't know what you mean," Simmons said helplessly.

"Do I have to spell it out for you?" Inman asked impatiently. "Was he breathing hard like he'd been running from something? Did he look worried over something?"

Simmons reflected on the questions. "He did at that," he said, eager to please Inman. "It looked to me like he was breathing hard."

"Good." Inman looked pleased.

He and Daugherty walked up the stairs and paused before Huston's room. Inman listened at the door, then drew his gun. He rammed his boot heel against the doorknob. Most of these hotel locks were flimsy. The impact of his heel shattered it.

Inman threw open the door and bounded into the room. Huston was just sitting up in bed. He was in his underwear, and Daugherty thought his eyes were dazed with interrupted sleep.

"Where have you been for the last hour?" Inman roared.

It took a moment for Huston to analyze the question, then he frowned. "What right have you got to ask me that?"

"Every right," Inman said. Huston's gunbelt hung over the bedpost at the foot of the bed. Inman picked the gun out of its holster and sniffed at the muzzle.

"Hah," he gloated. "This gun has been fired recently. You want to tell me why?"

Huston was getting angry. It made his cheekbones stand out prominently. "I fired it late this afternoon. I was walking my dog just outside of town. I killed a rabbit for him."

"You hit a rabbit with a pistol shot?" Inman scoffed.

Huston got out of bed and stood. His hands were bunched. "That rabbit was sitting." He was so furious he trembled. "What business is it of yours?"

"It just became my business," Inman said coldly. "I'm arresting you for the murder of Brad Cummings."

That stunned Huston. His mouth sagged, and for a moment, he couldn't find anything to say. "You're crazy," he stammered.

"Am I? We'll find out pretty soon. Get dressed. You're coming with me."

He tensed as Huston's muscles bunched. "Try something, and I'll put a bullet in you."

"You've tried and convicted him already," Daugherty said bitterly.

# CHAPTER SEVENTEEN

Every place he went, people stopped Inman to compliment him on the quick apprehension of Cummings's murderer.

"Sure, he's guilty," he replied to the twentieth time the question was asked of him. "His gun was recently fired. He tried to look as though he had been sleeping. You know how he felt about Brad. Huston has those killer eyes. I noticed them the night he shot Dent. He'll hang for killing Brad." Each time, he shook his head sorrowfully over his last remark. "It's too bad the county has to feed him so long before he's tried. The circuit judge won't be in town for a couple of weeks."

The people's reaction was always the same. "Goddam shame," they would say passionately. "Damned shame he doesn't have to pay now. This town has had enough of those Hustons. Something ought to be done right now."

"My feelings exactly," Inman would say before he moved on. He moistened a cigar and thrust it into his mouth. His newfound ability to stir people up and turn them in any direction he wanted them to go pleased him. He was carefully laying out a fuse that would set off an explosion that would take care of Gradie Huston for good. All he had to do was to pick out the right time to light the match to that fuse. Tonight, he pondered. Maybe that was a little soon. But tomorrow night at the latest.

Daugherty looked at the tray he carried from the restaurant across the street. Gradie had barely picked at the food.

"Damn it, Gradie," Daugherty complained. "A cockroach couldn't live on what you've eaten. This is the third meal you've hardly touched."

Gradie shook his head in weary resignation. "Not hungry. How's Hannah taking this, Cal?"

"Worried," Daugherty responded. "I've tried to show her that she doesn't have to worry, that Inman hasn't enough evidence to hold you."

"But you haven't been able to convince her," Gradie said quietly.

"No," Daugherty said gloomily. "I guess she's got every reason to fear the law here, after what it has done to her."

Daugherty set the tray on the floor and stretched his arm muscles. Worry was etching deep lines in his face.

"Gradie, Inman hasn't got a damned thing but guesswork," he burst out.

Gradie didn't notice how hard he gripped the bars, but his knuckles stood out in white relief. "Cal, it could be enough," he said evenly. "Have you talked to Letty?"

Daugherty shook his head. "I haven't tried, Gradie. Do you want me to see her?"

Gradie was tempted to say yes. He wanted Daugherty to tell Letty he didn't have anything to do with her father's death. He let the impulse slip away. If she believed that he was responsible, nothing would change her mind.

Gradie paced to the wall, whirled, and walked heavily back to where Daugherty stood. "Is the town pretty worked up?"

"They're getting rough," Daugherty said. "Everywhere I go, I see groups of people talking." He hesitated as though seeking a way to soften his words.

"And all of them accusing me," Gradie finished for him.

Daugherty sighed. "That's about it, Gradie."

For the first time, Gradie asked him a direct question. "Do you think I did it?"

"Damn it, no," Daugherty said savagely. "If you felt like killing Cummings, you wouldn't have waited that long. And you wouldn't have shot him in the back."

"Thanks," Gradie said gruffly. He couldn't stand still, and he took a few more restless steps.

"Why is Inman so dead set against you?" Daugherty asked.

Gradie managed a wry grin. "That doesn't make him any different from everybody else. I knew Slaughter felt that way, but I always thought it was because he killed Jonse. I guess some of his dislike for me rubbed off on Inman."

"It has to be more than that," Daugherty said stubbornly. "A couple of times, I heard Brad giving Slaughter and Inman hell. I wasn't close enough to hear why. Was Brad rough enough on one of them to make one want to kill him?" He grimaced. "Slaughter's shoulder rules him out. But what about Inman? Inman was at the church last night."

Gradie's eyes widened. "You sure of that?"

Daugherty nodded. "I'm sure. I heard Letty ask him where he'd gone. She was looking for him when somebody ran in to the church and announced Cummings had been shot." His eyes narrowed in sudden, intense thought. "I found him clear over on the other side of town. Was he trying to stay away as far as he could get from the spot where Cummings was killed?"

He saw the lighting in Gradie's face and warned, "That doesn't prove anything, Gradie."

"No," Gradie agreed. "But it could be a signpost. God knows, I haven't seen one until now. Slaughter and Inman were in my room. I saw them come out of the hotel. Simmons admitted they'd been up to my room. I searched it and found five hundred dollars, five brand-new bills. That money's still up there. I just changed its hiding place. Slaughter tore that room apart. He looked crazy when he couldn't find it."

Daugherty's voice trembled with a new excitement. "You didn't say anything about that."

Gradie shrugged. "What good would it have done? Who would admit they'd had a hand in it. Brad wanted me jailed for stealing his money. I can imagine he went wild when he heard his money was gone. How much hell did he raise in demanding that Slaughter and Inman get that money back?"

Daugherty drove his fist into his palm. "That explains one thing," he muttered.

Gradie's eyebrows rose, and Daugherty explained. "Inman went straight up to your room without asking Simmons for the room's number. I wondered about it."

The road sign was growing more legible, but it still didn't have Inman's name on it.

"I knew Cummings wanted me run out of town," Gradie said. "I knew that money had to be his. Slaughter and Inman didn't have that kind of money. You didn't hear Cummings talking about his lost money?"

Daugherty's face wrinkled in thought. "I did hear Brad yelling something about money the last time I heard them arguing. They shut up when they saw me."

Gradie couldn't help the faint thrust of hope he felt. "Cummings could be accusing them of taking that money. How much pressure did he put on Inman?" His face was heavy with thought. "Maybe he didn't believe they put that money in my room. Did he accuse Inman of taking it the night he was killed?"

"That's it," Daugherty exclaimed. "That ties everything together." There was no answering enthusiasm in Gradie's face. "What's wrong with that figuring?"

"Guesswork, Cal. Just guesswork," Gradie said despondently. "How far do you think that story would get in a court?"

Daugherty's face fell. "Not far, I guess," he muttered. He was silent a long moment. "But my God, doesn't it give us a direction in which to look?"

Gradie's eyebrows rose again. "We?"

"You're damned right," Daugherty said fiercely. "I'll watch Inman. We've got time. Something will turn up."

Daugherty felt far more assurance than Gradie did. So far, everything was working in Inman's favor. Gradie had knocked Cummings down, and added to that was the town's dislike of a Huston. Even Gradie shooting that rabbit was working for Inman.

"Maybe," he said listlessly.

Daugherty started to pick up the tray, and Gradie said, "I wish you'd do a couple of things for me, Cal."

"Name them," Daugherty said gruffly.

Gradie pulled what money he had remaining from his pocket

and handed it to Daugherty. "See that Hannah gets everything she needs. And feed Dog for me, will you?" He couldn't help the rush of despondency sweeping over him. There wasn't enough money to go very far.

"You didn't have to ask, Gradie. I've already seen Hannah and fed your dog." Daugherty managed a faint grin. "Hungry brute, isn't he?"

Gradie tried to match Daugherty's grin. "He sure is."

Daugherty picked up the tray. "He accepts food from me, but he's looking for you. I wish I could bring him in here, but I'm afraid to."

That put a savage animation in Gradie's face. "Don't," he said. Inman had already made one threat against Dog. Gradie didn't want to give him a chance to carry out that threat.

"I've got to take this tray back, Gradie. Then I want to make another round of the town. I'd like to keep abreast of—" He stopped helplessly.

Gradie knew why Daugherty stopped. He already knew what he faced. Painting it more vividly wouldn't do him any good.

"To see how far the town's fired up, Cal?" Gradie asked evenly.

"Something like that," Daugherty replied. "I won't be gone long."

Daugherty looked back from the door. Gradie still gripped those bars. There was too much strain in his face.

Gradie Huston was on everybody's mind. The more people thought about him, the more enflamed they became. The town was ready to blow. All it needed was a small push.

Inman turned a corner, and ahead of him was the largest group he had seen in the past two hours. There were at least forty people gathered here. He pushed his way to the center of the group. Haines was doing all the talking. Inman admitted Haines was pretty good at stirring everybody up, but giving Haines a little help wouldn't hurt.

Inman held up his palms until he had their attention. Several torches put queer, flickering lights on those enraged faces. Caleb Jones offered Inman a bottle, and Inman said, "Don't mind if I do." He let a generous drink slide down his throat, then handed the bottle back. This wasn't the only bottle he noticed passing hands.

"I guess he ate his three meals today," Haines said fiercely.

"Ever know of a Huston who wasn't hungry?" Inman said. He shook his head. "In a couple of weeks, he's going to put away a lot of food."

A growl started among the crowd and swelled. Sounds like a pack of wild dogs, Inman thought. "Too bad Judge Kleber doesn't get here tomorrow."

"Why should we wait on him?" Haines yelled. The growl grew to a roar. Haines had everybody with him.

"It's got to be done legally," Inman said judiciously.

"Why?" Haines demanded. "If we took care of him like we should, it'd save a lot of taxpayer money, wouldn't it?"

Inman considered that. "I've got to admit it would. But boys, you can't be asking me to turn him over to you."

"Why not?" a dozen voices shouted. "You think he's guilty, don't you?"

Inman held up his hands until he got silence. "There's no doubt of that. But dammit, my badge says I've got to protect him until he gets a fair trial."

"He's had all the trial he needs. He's guilty," Haines insisted. "There's only one thing to do. Lynch him!"

The answering roar of approval filled Inman with satisfaction. He had steered this along real good. There wasn't a dissenting voice among them. Now, all he had to do was to step aside.

He held up placating hands. "Now, wait just a minute, boys. I ain't saying you're wrong, and I ain't saying you're right. We've got to do some more talking about this." Just a few more words, Inman thought; until he was sure nothing could turn them back, or stop them. He didn't know what that damned fool Daugherty would do. Maybe something crazy like trying to block this crowd. Throw a little more fuel on the fire to be sure that nothing would dampen it, then it didn't matter what Daugherty tried to do.

Daugherty wondered where everybody was as he covered one street after another. All day long, he had seen small groups of men talking together. Where were those groups now? Had those men moved to the saloons to continue drinking while they talked? He hoped not. Hard drinking would only make matters worse. Liquor eased very few tempers, it only agitated them more.

Daugherty came around a corner, and his question was answered by the mob ahead of him. He pulled back hastily into a shadow, letting it envelope him. Some of the words were indistinguishable, just sounds of anger. But when a voice was raised, he heard it plain enough. His eyes smoldered as he listened to Inman. Inman always pitched his voice loud enough. He wanted everybody in this crowd to hear him. Goddam bastard, Daugherty raged inwardly. Instead of trying to calm this crowd, he was only encouraging them.

Daugherty stiffened as he heard the words, "Lynch him!" and the responsive, answering roar.

Inman held up placating hands. "Now, wait just a minute, boys. I ain't saying you're right, and I ain't saying you're wrong. We've got to do some more talking about this."

Daugherty wanted to tear into that crowd. He had something to tell these people, all the things he and Gradie had talked about, the things that pointed at Inman. The wild impulse slowly faded. He realized how foolish that would be. He wouldn't get a dozen words out of his mouth before they swarmed him under. They had gone too far to listen to reason.

Daugherty felt the sticky trickle of sweat, running out of his armpits. The fuse was lit and running wild. In a few more minutes, everything would blow sky high.

A dozen implausible solutions ran through his mind to be discarded as quickly as they entered. He could run back to the jail, barricade the door, and try to stand off this mob. Even if he let Gradie free to help him, they couldn't last long. Dropping some of the men in that mob would only enflame them that much more.

"Oh, God," he groaned. He turned and backed away out of the shadow, resisting the impulse to run. That would only draw attention. He had to do some sane thinking.

A block away from the mob, he hastened his pace. He couldn't hear them now, but he imagined he could. Now, he knew where he was going, what he was going to do.

He hurried into the livery stable. Sawyer wasn't there, and he sighed with relief. That solved a small, nagging problem. There was no need to think of some excuse to draw Sawyer away. Sawyer was probably with that mob.

He found Eagle in the fourth stall. Dog whined at his entrance, and Daugherty wasted a moment trying to soothe him.

"You can't go, Dog. It'd be dangerous for you to be running around tonight."

Daugherty hastily saddled Eagle and led him into the runway. He mounted and rode out into the street. The sweat ran faster. It was odd how it made him feel cold and clammy.

He rode Eagle into the alley back of the jail and ground-reined him, praying the horse would stay there.

Daugherty groaned as he remembered the back door to the jail was locked. He didn't have the keys. He ran back down the alley and around to the front of the building. At the front door he paused a moment to listen. He thought he heard voices in the distance, but as distraught as he was, he could be imagining anything.

He ran into the building and unlocked the back door. Then he turned to Gradie's cell and unlocked the door, throwing it wide.

Gradie looked at him stupefied. "What—"

"Don't argue with me," Daugherty said fiercely. "There's a lynch mob coming. Damn it, I saw and heard it. Don't stand there."

# CHAPTER EIGHTEEN

Gradie's face was blank as though he was incapable of thinking.

Daugherty reached into the cell and yanked him out. "Gradie," he implored. "You've got to move. I don't know how much time you've got. Eagle's in back of the building. Don't you understand?" he said frantically. "Inman's got that mob thinking of a rope. They'll be here any minute. I thought of trying to stand them off, Gradie. But that's no good. Nothing would stop them in the mood they're in."

That familiar stubbornness was molding Gradie's jaw. "And leave you here to face them?" he asked quietly.

Daugherty pulled out his gun and handed it to him. "I thought of that, too. Rap me over the head. Damn it!" His voice was getting shrill. "I've got to live in this town. When they find you gone, do you want them to turn on me?"

The agony of indecision was in Gradie's eyes. "I can't do that, Cal."

"You'd better," Daugherty said with brutal directness. "Who's going to look after Hannah and Dog, if you're not around?"

Gradie's hand tightened on the gun butt. Daugherty was right. He was thinking better than Gradie was. Gradie gulped hard, and his mouth was suddenly dry.

He forced his tongue to say, "Tell her I'll send for her and Dog as soon as I can."

Gradie raised the gun, and his hand shook noticeably. How hard did he hit to knock Daugherty unconscious and not injure him seriously? A gun barrel could break a man's skull.

The gun barrel swept down, catching Daugherty just above the ear. Daugherty's breath exploded out of him. His eyes rolled up into his head, and his legs buckled. He spilled onto the floor, his arms sprawling out ahead of him.

The skin above the ear was split, and the first thin line of blood strengthened, until it flowed down across Daugherty's cheek. Gradie bent over him. Daugherty was unconscious, but his breathing sounded steady enough to Gradie. The bleeding worried him, but he didn't have time to do anything about it. If Daugherty was right in what he thought would happen, he wouldn't be left unattended long.

He thrust Daugherty's gun into his waistband and hurried to the rear door. He opened it and slipped outside. His breathing came hard and rapid. He whipped his head about as he caught the sound. That was a volume of voices, filled with ominous threat, headed this way. Daugherty had timed this almost too well.

"Cal, I'll make it up some way," Gradie muttered. He threw the reins over Eagle's head and sprang into the saddle. He heard a new sound and for a moment couldn't place its source. The clog in Gradie's throat released, and he could breathe again. He had been looking too high off the ground. Dog bounded at his right leg, its slobbering whining showing his delight.

Gradie held out his arms. "Get up here, Dog. You've jumped it before."

Dog's body slammed into Gradie, its impact making Gradie reel in the saddle. His arms wrapped about Dog, and that long, wet tongue licked his face. A piece of rope dangled from Dog's neck.

Gradie hugged him tight, then held him against his hip with one arm. He lifted the reins with his free hand. "Time to get out of here, Dog."

He kept Eagle to a fast walk. That shouting sounded much closer to the jail now. It wasn't hard to visualize that surging mob pouring into the building.

Gradie rode out of the alley and crossed the street, not hesitating to look about him. His skin was tight in the anticipation of a yell that would mean discovery, and his teeth were set hard as he waited for the report of a gun followed by a bullet smashing into him. He kept Eagle down to that walk, though he wanted to give him his head. Carrying Dog was enough to draw attention to him, if anybody was around. He wanted no running horse to worsen the interest directed his way.

Three blocks were covered before he gave Eagle his head. Surely, it was safe to make a run for safety now.

He kept Eagle at a hard pace until Abilene fell well behind him. He let up the pressure on Eagle and said in an unbelieving voice, "Dog, we made it."

Dog whined and licked Gradie's face.

Maybe a pursuit would be organized, but that didn't bother Gradie too much. He had a big start, and it was dark. Elation kept bubbling within him until he was filled with it. One moment he had been hopelessly trapped, the next he was free. He owed Daugherty a tremendous debt. He couldn't even begin to think of how to start paying it.

Gradie kept looking behind him and saw no signs of pursuit. He could relax now and think of other things, like being run out of Abilene. His mouth twisted. That would have made Cummings completely happy, but he hadn't lived long enough to see it happen.

From Cummings Gradie's thoughts went to Letty. He wondered what she would do. She was all alone now. The sad loneliness welled up within him. He remembered the warm, good feeling he felt each time he saw her. That feeling had started in childhood and had never weakened. Under different circumstances that feeling might have developed into something stronger and more powerful.

He shook his head, trying to banish such thoughts. Such indulgent thoughts were foolish. He excused himself. Since he would probably never see her again, he had a right to all the sad thoughts in the world.

His eyes widened at a new thought. The direction he was taking would pass within two miles of the Cummings place. He could safely stop and tell Letty that he had nothing to do with the killing of her father. He owed himself that much, he argued. It was unbearable to think of her accusing him from now on.

Gradie cursed himself as he took the turnoff to the Cummings house. But a brief stop wouldn't be that risky. If Inman did organize a posse, he didn't have the slightest idea of what direction Gradie had taken.

A light was on in the house when Gradie pulled up before it. The bunkhouse behind the house was dark. A cowhand had enough filling his days without trying to stretch them after dark. Gradie imagined Letty had many troubled thoughts that would keep sleep from coming too easily to her.

Gradie pulled up before the tie rack, tossed Dog onto the ground, climbed down and wrapped his reins about the pole. He bent and roughed up Dog's ears. "You can't go in," he said in a low voice. Maybe he couldn't, either. Maybe Letty would look at him with only loathing in her eyes. Those thoughts hurt.

"You stay around here close," he told Dog.

Peering through the front window, Gradie saw Letty walking restlessly about the room. Gradie was right about troubled thoughts keeping her from resting.

The hollow in his stomach grew and drawing a deep breath did nothing to dispel the feeling. Letty might not even listen to him, he thought miserably. But he was going to tell her the truth. But what if she screamed and aroused the hands in the bunkhouse. There was that possibility. He was still going to try to explain to her what had happened. If the aroused cowboys did pour out of the bunkhouse, he would still have a start on them. He hesitated a long moment, evaluating the risk from all angles. It was a useless waste of time. He knew full well what he was going to do.

Gradie tapped on the door, then again, not really giving her time to answer his first tap.

My God, how a second could stretch into an eternity. The waiting pulled him tight. He started to tap again, then the door opened.

Letty stared at him. Gradie could read nothing in her eyes, no loathing, no hating, no emotion of any kind.

"Letty," he said awkwardly. "I had to see you. I wanted you to know I didn't kill your father."

She reached out, grabbed his hand, and pulled him inside. She shut the door behind him and leaned against it as though to bar outside interference by the weight of her body.

"I never thought you did, Gradie," she said steadily.

Dumfounded, he stared at her. He heard what she said, but was too stunned to fully comprehend.

When he relaxed a little and tried to grin, he realized how tightly his jaws had been clamped together.

"I thought—I mean—" He stopped and drew a deep breath. He was babbling like a fool. He drew another breath and had control again.

"There wasn't any love between your father and me, Letty," he said flatly. He shook his head. "That wasn't enough to make me shoot him in the back."

Her eyes never left his face. He thought some of that drawn, haggard look was lessening. She believed him. His throat was no longer tight, and he felt like grinning.

"What makes you believe me, Letty? Everybody else is against me."

She made a helpless gesture. "I—I just knew. After what Papa did to your family, and you didn't retaliate, I guess that made me know."

Her eyes widened, and fear crept into them. "Gradie, how did you get out of jail? I know Inman didn't just release you. The last I heard, he was talking against you all over town."

"I broke jail," he said and smiled at the increasing terror in her face. "In a way, I guess I did, Letty. Daugherty helped me. Cal is one of the few people who believe in me." Briefly, he sketched his talk with Daugherty about Inman. "It points to Inman, Letty," he said woodenly. He shrugged. "But there's no proof. Inman stirred up a mob to lynch me. Daugherty told me he heard him. He insisted I leave. When he said 'lynch mob' that convinced me."

"But won't they blame him?" she cried.

"That worried me, too. I rapped him over the head with a gun barrel. He had Eagle out in back for me." At her tremor of apprehension he said quietly, "All Cal's idea. I knocked him unconscious, but he's all right. I checked to be sure. He said he had to live in that town. As crazy as that mob was, they might have put Cal in my place, if they found out he set me free." Worry etched frowning lines in his forehead. "I sure hope he knows what he's talking about."

"This means you have to run, doesn't it?" That was a despairing note in her voice.

"It does," he said gravely. "Nobody would listen to me, or even to Cal. Everybody's made up their minds. With Inman prodding them along, they're not going to change their opinion. That's why I had to see you, to tell you I didn't do it."

A shudder ran through her. "Will Inman let it stop there?"

Gradie knew what she meant. He could be on the run for the rest of his life. His smile was a poor, strained imitation. "It's better than sitting in that jail, waiting for them, isn't it?"

"Oh, Gradie. Why does it have to be this way? After Papa died, I hoped you could stay. Gradie, what am I going to do?"

He understood the despair in her voice. She was alone with the huge job of keeping the Cummings place going. No wonder the weight of that prospect was crushing her.

"I wish to God I could stay and help you, Letty," he said softly.

Her eyes brimmed with tears. "I wouldn't ask for anything else, Gradie." Her face was turned up to him, and all the longing in the world was in those eyes.

He did the only natural thing. He took a long step forward and took her in his arms. There wasn't the slightest resistance in her. He bent his head, and her mouth willingly met his.

Gradie didn't know how long that kiss lasted; maybe a few seconds or an eternity. He lifted his head and stared wonderingly, filled with the rapture of a brand-new discovery. His laugh was too shaky to sound normal.

"Letty, I'm in love with you. I guess I always have been."

Her fingers caressed his cheek. "I knew a long time ago, Gradie."

He kissed her again. The loneliness came back, making it doubly hard to say what he had to say.

"I've got to go, Letty,"

"I know," she whispered. Her voice was close to breaking.

"There's one thing I want to ask you. Will you look after

Hannah? Dr. Barnes said she needed a long rest before she can travel. I'll send for her after I get settled." A hope flashed through that loneliness. Maybe Letty would join him. The futility of that hope got through to him. He could offer her nothing but the hardships of a wanted man's future.

She buried her face against his chest and sobbed. She knew the hopelessness of it without him saying a word.

She raised her head, and tears sparkled in her eyes and slowly trickled down her cheeks. "Oh, Gradie," she wailed. "Will I ever see you again?"

"I don't know," he answered honestly.

He knew he should leave, but he couldn't. God, didn't he have the right to a few more minutes with her? But each passing minute only made it that much harder to go.

He finally pushed her away from him. "I've got to go, Letty."

She nodded numb acceptance and turned away. Her back was toward him when he reached the door. He wanted to go back and touch her once more. Futility made him sick with rage and despair. He opened the door and stepped outside, closing the door softly behind him.

Did the closed door muffle her crying? He didn't know if his ears or his imagination was playing him tricks.

Gradie's eyes were hot and stinging as he walked to Eagle. He looked about him. Where was that damned dog? He shook his head impatiently, not daring to call Dog, or spend any more time looking for him.

He put his boot in the stirrup and reached up for the horn.

A gun muzzle jabbed into the small of his back. "Just make one wrong move, Huston. Just one."

Gradie stiffened, and his mouth went dry. How well he knew that goddam voice.

# CHAPTER NINETEEN

Inman led the mob into the jail. They crowded in after him, shoving and pushing to be the first inside. Their boots scraped against the floor, and their faces were ugly with anticipation.

Inman stopped short and said, "What the hell?"

The mob surged up against him, and he threw out his arms to hold them back.

Daugherty sat on the floor, holding his head in his hands. Blood oozed from between his fingers, staining the back of his hands.

Inman rushed to the cell, passing Daugherty. The cell door was open. The longer he stared, the blacker his fury grew. That damned Huston was gone.

He returned and pushed through the ring of men who now surrounded Daugherty. "Huston's gone," he yelled. "Daugherty let him get away."

"Shut up," Inman screamed at the babbling voices. He thrust his face close to Daugherty's making no effort to help him to his feet.

"You let him go," he screamed again.

Pain twisted Daugherty's face as he attempted to stand. It took a second try before he made it. He walked a few unsteady steps and dropped into a chair. "Jesus," he moaned. "My head's coming off."

Angry faces crowded in around him, all asking the same question. Why had he let Huston go? Why?

"I didn't," he protested stoutly. "Huston was lying on his cot. I called to him, but he didn't answer. I tried to arouse him for several minutes. I thought he was dead. I went in and bent over him. He jerked my gun out of its holster. He forced me out of the cell, then hit me. That's all I remember."

Inman looked insane. "Of all the goddam fool stunts," Inman raged.

"He's derelict in his duty," Haines said shrilly.

Inman was slowly getting a hold on himself. He glared at Haines. "What do you want to do with him? Hang him in Huston's place?"

Haines's eyes wavered, then broke before Inman's fierce stare. "Something's got to be done," he mumbled. "We can't just let Huston get away."

Inman's thoughts were clicking again. Maybe this was just as well. Huston was gone, and this time, for sure. Huston's running was the final proof of his guilt. Abilene would never see Gradie Huston again. Inman would settle for what he had.

"Where do we look?" he asked harshly. "Which direction do we take?"

He glared at the men around him, and none of them could meet his eyes. That solid feeling of satisfaction filled Inman again. Outside of hanging Huston, he couldn't have asked for things to turn out better. The town was satisfied that Huston was Cummings's killer.

The former mass hysteria of the crowd melted away. Men muttered instead of yelling, and feet shuffled restlessly on the floor.

"Clear out of here," Inman yelled in sudden impatience. "I'll get out some feelers for Huston. When I get a lead, I'll come after all of you quick enough." He was sure he wouldn't hear of Huston again. Huston wouldn't stop running for a long way, maybe not until he crossed the border.

He jerked his head toward Daugherty. "Two of you take him to Doc Barnes and get him patched up." Disgust filled his voice, as he looked at Daughtery. "I don't want a damned deputy like that in my office."

A strong approval of his decision ran through the room. It was difficult for Inman to keep a grin off his face. That was another problem easily solved. Now, he wouldn't get any disagreement from the townspeople when he fired Daugherty.

Two men helped Daugherty toward the door.

Sawyer was one of the last men to leave the office, and Inman stopped him with a question. "Sawyer, have you been away from the stable all evening?"

Sawyer caught the censure in Inman's face and voice. He hung his head and shuffled his feet. He tried to build up a righteous indignation. "Sure, I was away for a little while. Damn it, Hebb, I didn't like him any better than the rest of you did. I wanted to see he got what was coming to him."

Inman spat on the floor and growled, "You left a way open for him to get out of town. Hell yes, you did." He yelled to drown Sawyer's gathering protest. "He slipped in and got his horse while you were gone."

Sawyer looked startled. "My God, Hebb, I didn't mean to do anything like that."

"Skip it," Inman said roughly. "It's done. Get my horse saddled."

Eagerness flooded Sawyer's face. "You going after Huston alone, Hebb?"

Inman wanted to snort at that ridiculous question, but he could use it to his advantage. "I'm going to do some looking around," he said casually. Hell no, he wasn't going to spend any time looking for Huston. Let Sawyer spread what Inman told him around town. People would look at each other and say admiringly, "That Inman never gives up, does he?" That made him want to laugh. He had this town right in the palm of his hand. What he was going to do was to ride out and see Letty Cummings. He would never have a better chance to improve his standing with her. He would bring her the news that now there was no doubt Gradie Huston shot her father in the back.

Sawyer babbled all the way to the stable. Inman paid little attention to what he said. He occasionally answered with a grunt or a nod. His pleasure grew at thinking of how Letty's eyes would shine. This time, that crusty, old bastard wouldn't be around to say he could or could not talk to her.

# The Grudge

Sawyer lingered a moment before he went after Inman's horse. Inman's patience broke. "Will you get your ass moving?" he roared. "Huston could cross two counties before you bring me my horse."

That made Sawyer move with alacrity. Inman grinned sourly as he watched him go down the runway. He hadn't thought Sawyer had that much hurry in him.

Sawyer brought back the saddled horse, and Inman mounted. Sawyer looked up at him. "Here's wishing you all the luck in the world."

"Sure," Inman said and rode out. He wished the same thing for himself but regarding a different matter than Sawyer meant.

He was suddenly impatient to get out to the Cummings place, and he kicked the horse into faster motion. The feeling that this was going to be a big night rushed over him.

He hummed a tuneless song all the way out to the Cummings house. His face darkened as he saw the horse tied up before the house. Who was visiting Letty tonight?"

Fifty yards from the tie rack, Inman tethered his horse to a bush. He crept up to the house and peeked into a window. He thought he would explode at what he saw. That worthless Huston had his arms around Letty.

Inman's scowl slowly faded into a cruel grin. The night was still turning out right for him. He was going to bring Huston's body back. If Letty had any grief over that, it would be short; particularly, when she learned Huston had lied to her.

Inman moved quietly to a patch of shadow a few yards from Huston's horse. His teeth bared as he tasted the savory thought. He could visualize Huston's absolute terror when he stepped up behind him. Huston wouldn't have to suffer that terror long, he thought viciously.

Inman didn't know how long he waited, but it seemed a month before Huston came out of the house. His shoulders were bowed, and he moved like an old, tired man. He looked back at the house once before he reached his horse.

Huston put a boot in the stirrup and grabbed the horn.

Inman straightened and moved soundlessly to him. He jabbed the gun viciously into the small of Huston's back.

"Just make one wrong move, Huston," he said savagely. "Just one."

# CHAPTER TWENTY

Gradie's legs felt like string. He was sure they would have crumbled on him, if he hadn't a hold of the horn.

"You damned murderer," Inman said. "Turn around."

Gradie slowly complied.

Inman looked at the gun tucked in Gradie's waistband. "Take that gun out and drop it on the ground. Easy," he snapped.

Gradie had a fleeting impulse to grab for his gun, then realized how foolish the motion would be. Inman's gun was leveled on him. Inman would kill him before he touched the gun.

He could read the inevitable in Inman's eyes. It doesn't make any difference when it happened, he thought dully, now or a few minutes later. Inman was going to kill him.

Gradie clung to the few seconds he might have left. Slowly, he pulled the gun out with thumb and forefinger and dropped it on the ground. Stalling for time, he said desperately, "You know I'm not the murderer, Inman." He spoke with a degree of calmness that surprised him. "You know who really shot Cummings."

Inman's gun never wavered. "What are you talking about?" he growled.

"You killed him, Inman. You shot him in the back because he was threatening you. You knew you'd never get back in the sheriff's office without him backing you."

Inman didn't make an audible sound, but Gradie was sure Inman's lips twitched. "Damned smart, ain't you?" Inman jeered.

Gradie wanted to jolt Inman further, and he almost let foolish words slip out. He choked them back just in time. If only he could threaten Inman with the knowledge that other people knew the real killer— How badly he wanted to say that he had told Letty who killed her father. Neither could he say that he had talked it over with Cal Daugherty. Naming those two people wouldn't keep Inman from killing him. It would only focus Inman's attention on Letty and Daugherty, and Gradie knew he was fully capable of killing them both. No, he couldn't save himself, but he might save them. Perhaps together, the two could put pressure on Inman so that he couldn't escape.

It won't do me any good, Gradie thought drearily. If there was any satisfaction in the fact that Inman might not go free, Gradie couldn't find it.

Gradie was suddenly, horribly tired; too tired to really be concerned over future consequences. "What are you going to do now, Inman?"

Inman's chuckle was an ugly, grating sound. "Are you hoping I'd take you back and lock you up again? Do you think I'm that crazy, Huston. Hell, I couldn't risk you getting away the second time, could I?"

Inman aimed the pistol at Gradie's head. "Where do you want it, Huston? Between the eyes, or in the belly?" He enjoyed his cruel taunting. "I'd better make it between the eyes. In the belly might let you do a little talking. You'd try to lie some more."

Gradie cursed him in a dull, flat voice. He called him every ugly thing he knew, hoping to fire Inman's anger until his finger tightened on the trigger and ended this nightmare.

Inman was only amused. "What's the matter, Huston? You want to make it fast? I'm getting a kick out of watching you squirm."

He held the gun pointed steadily at Gradie's eyes. "Just think. You'll never know when it's coming. Is the sweat running down into your boots yet?"

Inman chuckled again, and the sound scraped across Gradie's raw nerve ends.

"You don't realize it, Inman, but everything's going to fall in on you. Everybody can see through you. Tomorrow, they'll be spitting on you."

Where the obscenties and curses didn't touch Inman, this last got through to him. "Shut up, damn you," he raged. "You want it right now? Well, you're going to get—"

At that moment, as if he could understand the meaning of Inman's words, Dog launched himself into the spring that would carry him into Inman. At the last split-second, Inman heard something, or some instinct warned him. He whipped his head about, trying to spot what threatened him. He was too late to do anything to stop Dog's charge out of the darkness. His cry of alarm was garbled and broken. Dog's bound hit Inman on the right side. Inman staggered, but didn't go down. He whirled, swinging his gun about, trying to train it on the animal. Dog hit him in the chest, bowling him over. A startled squawk tore out of Inman's mouth, then Dog's savage growling drowned it out.

Dog was a whirlwind of fury, his fangs slashing at Inman. Inman kept trying to get an aim on that streak of light, and Dog was in and out before Inman could train his sights on him. Vicious fangs ripped shirt and flesh alike from elbow to wrist. Inman screamed in terror and pain. His arm flew up to ward off another charge, his hand opened, and the gun flew out of it. He tried to roll to escape the fury that threatened to tear out his throat. He kicked at Dog and flailed at him with both hands, but Inman couldn't do all three things successfully at once.

Gradie darted forward and scooped up Inman's gun. He moved two more steps, bent, and retrieved his own gun. He thrust one weapon into his waistband and held the other in his hand.

Inman couldn't roll fast enough to keep Dog off of him, and he couldn't hit Dog with his fists. Each useless effort tore a grunting sob out of him. His shirt hung in tatters, and blood, looking black in the dark, was on his face, arms, and chest.

"Stop him," he moaned. "Stop him. He'll kill me."

Gradie's relief made him lightheaded. Inman had earned what he was getting. Gradie didn't give a damn whether or not Dog tore him to pieces.

The noise of the struggle must have reached Letty. Gradie wasn't aware she was out of the house until she came running to him.

"Gradie," she cried. "What's happening?"

Gradie threw out an arm to check her. "It's Dog, ripping into Inman," he said soberly. "Inman was going to shoot me."

Letty looked at the bloody figure on the ground and shuddered. "Gradie," she whispered. "You've got to stop him."

It was hard to agree with her, and it took a long moment before Gradie slowly nodded.

"Dog," he called. "Back."

Dog was too engrossed to hear Gradie, or else he had no intention of letting go of his prey.

Gradie darted in, made a sweep at the rope dangling from Dog's neck, and caught it. Dog's lunge almost pulled Gradie off his feet. Gradie set himself against the brute power and yanked on Dog. He dragged Dog a few feet away from Inman, yelling at the top of his voice, "Dog, down. Down."

Dog lunged again at the moaning man. Gradie thought his arm would be yanked out of the socket.

"Damn it, Dog. Do you hear me? I said down."

Dog settled back on his haunches. His lips were pulled back from his fangs, and the snarling never stopped.

Inman's moaning broke up his words. "Help me," he begged. "I'm bleeding to death." He put his hands against the ground and started to rise.

"Try to get up, and I'll turn him loose again," Gradie said.

His voice was encouragement to Dog, for the animal stood and lunged again. Gradie wrestled him back into place. "Damn it, Dog," he complained. "Will you behave?"

Inman settled back on the ground. "You can't just stand there and let me bleed to death."

"Try me," Gradie invited.

He turned his head toward Letty. "He didn't intend to arrest me, Letty. He was going to shoot me right here. He had a gun pointed at me." He could grin now with more feeling. "Dog didn't like that."

His voice hardened as he spoke again to Inman. "Tell Letty what you told me."

Inman's eyes shifted. "I don't know what you mean."

"You'd better remember in a hurry," Gradie said grimly. "Or

I'm turning Dog loose again." He bent over the animal as though to take the rope from his neck.

Terror twisted Inman's face. "No," he half screamed. "My God, you wouldn't do that."

"In about one second, you're going to find out." The grimness hadn't left Gradie's voice. "Tell her about her father, Inman." His voice crackled. "I mean right now."

For a moment, it looked as though Inman would defy him, then his eyes went to Dog's slathering fangs, and he whimpered.

"I shot Brad," he said sullenly. He looked at the stiffening in Letty's face and begged, "I had to do it. He said he'd see that I wouldn't wear the sheriff's badge long." His voice broke, and he sounded as though he was going to cry. "Don't you see? I had to do it."

Gradie was afraid she would cry. "Here now," he said softly. "It's almost all over."

She stared at him, her eyes seeming to grow bigger and bigger. "You won't have to run any more."

"Why, no," he said. "Inman's going to fill my place."

He pointed the gun into the air. Before he pulled the trigger he explained, "I want some more witnesses to hear him. I'm going to call your men."

Letty nodded in quick understanding.

Gradie pulled the trigger. Dog turned his head around and looked inquiringly at Gradie. "It's all right," Gradie assured him. He pulled the trigger again. That should bring the additional witnesses in a hurry.

Letty knelt beside Dog and wrapped her arms about his neck. "He grows more beautiful every day, doesn't he?"

Gradie looked at Dog judiciously. "I wouldn't go as far as to say that. But he sure grows on you."

Six men pounded around the corner of the house in various stages of undress. Two of them hadn't taken time to put on their shirts, and one was barefooted. Hostility and bewilderment was mixed in their faces as they looked at Gradie and Letty, then at the groveling figure on the ground.

"Miss Letty, are you all right?" the older one demanded.

159

"Just fine, Pike," she answered. Her voice was fresh and vibrant again. "Everything's under control. This is Gradie Huston."

That made Pike and a younger man uncomfortable. "Not the same—" Pike couldn't get the question out.

"One of the same Hustons," Letty said. "Pike, he didn't come here to quarrel with us." She pointed at the cringing figure on the ground. "Don't you recognize Sheriff Inman?"

She looked at the increasing scowl on the younger man's face. "What's troubling you, Ord?"

Ord stared at Inman, then at Gradie. "Huston's the one who shot Brad in the back. Why, dammit, he should be in jail." He looked around for agreement, and heads bobbed. Ord's voice picked up a notch in excitement. "I don't know what this Huston's told you, but you've got it all wrong."

Inman grabbed at a faint hope. "She is wrong. I tried to arrest Huston, and he sicked that dog on me. Help me—" He started to get up.

Dog snarled at his movement.

"Do you want me to turn him loose again, Inman?" Gradie asked softly. "Tell them what you told Letty and me."

Dog quivered with eagerness to get at Inman again. Gradie let out a little bit of the rope. That was all the encouragement Dog need to lunge forward again. Gradie almost lost his grip on the rope.

"Hold it, Dog," Gradie ordered. He wrestled with Dog and pulled him back. "Better tell them, Inman. I can't hold him much longer."

"Oh, God," Inman moaned. "Ain't any of you going to help me?"

"All right, Inman. If that's what you want," Gradie said.

Dog was fury incarnate again. Those fangs looked a foot long, and he slobbered.

"Oh, Jesus," Inman moaned, and his resistance collapsed. "I had to shoot Brad." His words were jerky as he related the incident. "Don't you see?" he implored. "I couldn't do anything else."

Letty's riders looked at one another, then at Gradie. All of their hostility was gone.

"Mister," Pike said gruffly, "you're damned lucky to have that dog."

"I'm kinda aware of it," Gradie said drily.

"What are we going to do with him?" Ord asked balefully.

Pike spat in Inman's direction. "I've got a few ideas."

"You're going to do nothing," Gradie said sharply.

Pike frowned at him. "You're not just going to turn him loose?"

"No," Gradie replied. "I'm going to turn him over to the town. They've been backing him pretty hard. I want everybody to get a good look at him."

Gradie grinned at their puzzled looks. "Will one of you ride into town and bring back Cal Daugherty? Oh yes, tell Cal I want him to bring about four of the leading citizens with him. I want all of them to listen to Inman's story."

"I'll go," Ord said eagerly.

"Take my horse," Gradie responded. "He's ready."

He listened to the receding hoofbeats. It was going to be quite a good stretch of time before Ord returned with Daugherty and the others. The way tonight turned out should pay Cal for that rap on the head. There wasn't another logical person in town to wear the sheriff's badge.

Inman stirred, and Dog snarled a warning.

"What will be done with him?" Pike asked.

"I imagine what Inman wanted for me," Gradie said gravely. His laugh rang out. "I won't be fretting too much over that."

Inman looked fearfully at Dog. "You can't keep me just laying here. I'm bleeding. I could lie here and die."

"That's where you'll stay," Gradie said unfeelingly. "I want to be sure you tell the same story to the townspeople."

"But I'm bleeding." Inman's voice cracked.

Pike spat at him again. "Real tough. Then you'd better pray you've got a lot of blood to leak out."

Letty turned toward the house.

"Letty—" Gradie stopped, seeking how to put what he wanted to say to her about what had happened, about the past, and the future.

"What is it?" she asked.

"I was just wondering where you were going," he said lamely.

She asked an odd question. "How long is it since Dog has been fed?"

Gradie stared at her, bewildered. "I don't know." His face brightened, as he realized why she was going to the house. He stooped and roughed Dog's ears. "Dog, I don't know which one brought the other luck. But it looks like things are going to be all right from now on."

Dog looked up and tried to lick Gradie's face.